"Don't f

Bryce said huskily. "I
started last night."

"But you were the one who broke it off," Carol
protested. His breath was warm on her cheek.

"And you know why," he said raggedly. "If I
hadn't, I'd have spent the night making love to
you."

"Is something different now?" His lips roamed
tenderly over her cheeks and forehead, and Carol
knew she sounded as breathless as she felt.

"Mmm-hmm." Bryce sounded breathless, too. "My
self-control is back in working order. Last night I
couldn't think straight."

Carol trailed kisses along his jaw. "I'm glad yours is
so strong," she murmured, "because mine is slipping
badly."

His moan was muffled against her lips as he covered
her mouth with his own.

Dear Reader:

The spirit of the Silhouette Romance Homecoming Celebration lives on as each month we bring you six books by continuing stars!

And we have a galaxy of stars planned for 1988. In the coming months, we're publishing romances by many of your favorite authors such as Annette Broadrick, Sondra Stanford and Brittany Young. Beginning in January, Debbie Macomber has written a trilogy designed to cure any midwinter blues. And that's not all—during the summer, Diana Palmer presents her most engaging heroes and heroines in a trilogy that will be sure to capture your heart.

Your response to these authors and other authors of Silhouette Romances has served as a touchstone for us, and we're pleased to bring you more books with Silhouette's distinctive medley of charm, wit and—above all—romance.

I hope you enjoy this book and the many stories to come. Come home to romance—for always!

Sincerely,

Tara Hughes
Senior Editor
Silhouette Books

PHYLLIS HALLDORSON

Return to Raindance

Silhouette *Romance*

Published by Silhouette Books New York

America's Publisher of Contemporary Romance

For Beth Tigner
A dear and true friend, who taught me to write
emotion, and who has listened to and critiqued every
manuscript I've written. Dedication above and
beyond the call. Thank you.

SILHOUETTE BOOKS
300 E. 42nd St., New York, N.Y. 10017

Copyright © 1988 by Phyllis Halldorson

ISBN: 0-373-08566-4

First Silhouette Books printing March 1988

SILHOUETTE, SILHOUETTE ROMANCE and colophon
are registered trademarks of the publisher.

America's Publisher of Contemporary Romance

Printed in the U.S.A.

Books by Phyllis Halldorson

Silhouette Romance

Temporary Bride #31
To Start Again #79
Mountain Melody #247
If Ever I Loved Again #282
Design for Two Hearts #367
Forgotten Love #395
Undercover Lover #456
To Choose a Wife #515
Return to Raindance #566

Silhouette Special Edition

My Heart's Undoing #290
The Showgirl and the Professor #368
Cross My Heart #430

PHYLLIS HALLDORSON,

like all her heroines, is as in love with her husband today as on the day they met. It is because she has
known so much love in her own life that her charac-
ters seem to come alive as they, too, discover the joys
of romance.

RAINDANCE, NEBRASKA

A fictitious town.

1. Raindance Inn
2. Carol's Childhood Home
3. Perkin's Home
4. Church
5. Bryce's Home
6. Trent Realty Co.
7. Bryce's Law Office

North Main St.

Main St.

Highway 20

Cedar St.

Park

1
2
3
4
5
6
7

Chapter One

With every passing mile the combination of anticipation and dread Carol Murphy was feeling increased. She was going home. But home was where Bryce still lived, and there would be no welcome for her there.

Her sandaled foot eased up on the gas pedal as the community water tower came into view, and her late-model red Jaguar slowed on the two-lane highway in northwestern Nebraska where traffic was practically nonexistent.

Carol had been born, raised, married and divorced, all within twenty years, in the small prairie town of Raindance. Eight years ago she'd left town alone, humiliated and heartbroken—one of the participants in a scandal that had rocked the whole state, even as it had broken up her marriage and brought shame to her proud, pioneer-stock parents. In disgrace she'd driven her elderly 1972 Chevrolet, the only thing salvaged from her shattered marriage, halfway across the country to Los Angeles, where her aunt and uncle had offered a haven.

Now, eight years older and light-years smarter, she had a master's degree from UCLA, a well-paying public relations job in the television industry and absolutely no desire to return to the scene of her pain and humiliation. Unfortunately she had no choice. Business affairs that only she could handle needed attention.

A highway sign that had been new when she left but was now weathered and faded announced: Raindance, Pop. 2,350. Apparently the population hadn't changed much, Carol thought as she followed Highway 20 into Raindance. The road ran east and west through the rural town, dividing it into halves with residences to the north and the business district to the south. There were a few houses in the southern area, too, but they were mostly older and run-down.

There were still no motels on the western side of town, so Carol kept driving until she was stopped at the one and only traffic light, where the highway intersected with Main Street.

Gazing around curiously as she waited for the light to change, she noted that a new courthouse stood next to the park on the northwest corner, the old white two-story apartment house on the northeast corner had been painted yellow, and one of the two gas stations on the south side of the intersection was now a convenience store with pumps.

The light turned green, and she glanced to her right as she drove on through the intersection. The four-block-long main business street didn't seem to have changed much, although she'd no doubt find that some of the stores had new occupants. A wave of nostalgia assailed her as she wondered if the old ice-cream parlor where the high-school kids used to gather was still in existence. Bryce had taken her there after the movie on their first date....

Her fingers curled tightly around the steering wheel as the old familiar ache gnawed at her nerve ends. No, she wasn't going to think about Bryce Garrett. It had taken her years to adjust to the pain of losing him, and she wasn't going to start it up all over again. She'd never stop loving him, but she'd finally learned to live without him. She'd even found a measure of peace, although the nagging guilt was always with her, somewhere deep below the surface of her cool, professional exterior.

If only... But her growing-up years had been a long series of "if onlys," and she knew that kind of thinking was a dead end. She couldn't change the past, but she didn't need to let it dictate her future. There was nothing for her in Raindance, and the more quickly she concluded her business and got away from here the better.

Almost at the eastern edge of town, Carol pulled up and stopped in front of the business office of the Raindance Inn, a motel that had been new eight years ago. Its brick exterior had survived the elements with little damage, and a large restaurant, whose neon sign proclaimed it Stan's Steak and Stein, had been constructed next door.

Unfortunately for her hopes of anonymity, the man behind the registration desk had gone to school with her from the first grade on. At first he eyed her uncertainly, but as soon as she wrote her name in the register his face lit up. "Carol Murphy! I knew you looked familiar, but it's been a long time."

Carol gave him her brightest smile. "Hello, Scooter. Yes it has been a long time. How are you?"

"Fine, fine—but I'm called Frank now. Finally grew out of Scooter. I'm manager here. Gee, this is a surprise. Will you be staying long?"

She took the key he handed her. "Only a few days. Great to see you, Sc—Frank."

When she reached her room, she shut the door behind her with something akin to relief and looked around. It was small but neat and clean, with matching blue-print spread and draperies, a portable television and a bathroom with a shower and tub. It was also air-conditioned—a necessity in the humid heat of the prairie in mid-July.

Carol glanced at her watch. It was almost two o'clock, and she was weary from driving steadily for three and a half long days, but the sooner she got to the business that brought her here, the sooner she could leave. She had a gut feeling that the heartbreak she'd left behind was still lurking in Raindance, and she wanted no part of it.

With a sigh she picked up the small booklet that seemed more like a pamphlet than a telephone directory and looked up the number of Thomas Trent Realty, a real estate agency new to the area since she'd lived here. The secretary informed her that Mr. Trent was out but would be back by three and would see her then.

She fully intended to shut the directory and put it away, but her undisciplined fingers riffled through the pages until they found the *G*'s. Garrett and Son, Accounting stood out in the bold black letters that distinguished the businesses from the residents. So Bryce and his father still owned their firm, and the phone number engraved in her memory hadn't changed. She felt a tightness in her throat, and as she closed the book and lowered it to the table she noticed that her hands were shaking.

By two forty-five Carol had showered and changed into a tailored yellow sleeveless linen dress and had plaited her heavy shoulder-length black hair into the neat, businesslike French braid she habitually wore to work. Her creamy light complexion and deep blue eyes, so unusual with raven hair, were a legacy from her Irish father and needed only a touch of blusher and a stroke of eyeliner to accentuate them.

If it wasn't so hot she'd walk the six or so blocks to the Main Street address. She needed the exercise after being cooped up in the car for so long, but with the temperature at more than a hundred and the high humidity she'd be wilted and soaked with perspiration by the time she got there. Reluctantly she climbed back in the Jaguar and started the powerful motor.

Thomas Trent was a nice-looking man of about forty, of medium height and build, but with prematurely gray hair that immediately set him apart. He stood as she entered his office, and she saw typical male admiration in his brown eyes as he extended his hand. "Carol," he said pleasantly, "I'm Tom. It's nice to finally meet you."

They'd gotten on a first-name basis through the letters they'd been exchanging over the past few weeks, and Carol took his hand and smiled. "Thank you. I feel like I know you already, but you didn't tell me you had such a lovely wife."

She turned to look at the pretty, slightly chubby, dark-haired woman who acted as receptionist and secretary. "Donna tells me you have a couple of sons."

He beamed with pride. "Yeah, they're eight and ten. Ornery little devils, but we like 'em." He motioned toward the chair beside her. "Please, sit down. Donna, hold the phone calls for a while."

Donna left, and Tom and Carol settled themselves comfortably. Thank goodness the office, too, was air-conditioned, a commodity not always as available in this small rural town as it was in the cities.

Tom opened a file on the desk in front of him. "So, has the town changed much since you've been gone? Understand it's been several years since you've been back."

Carol nodded. "Eight. It doesn't seem to have changed a great deal, but I just drove in about an hour ago, so I haven't seen much of it. Your business is new since then. How long have you been here?"

"Only about a year. I used to work for a large realty company in Lincoln, but Donna and I always wanted to be on our own, and when we heard that one of the two realtors here in Raindance had retired, we decided this was a good area. We like it here, and business is picking up. And speaking of business . . ." He flipped through the papers in the file. "What exactly is your mother objecting to? That property of hers out in the Sandhills has little value; it's undeveloped and not big enough for ranching. Seems to me that the offer my client has made for it is more than generous."

Carol leaned back in her chair. "I'm inclined to agree with you, but Mom's so sure that there's oil under that land."

"But that's nonsense—"

"Not necessarily. My grandfather had a geologist look at it, and he said that soil conditions and other things were right for oil. But Grandpa was never able to raise the money to sink a hole."

She waved a hand at his skeptical look. "I know, it's a long shot, but try to tell my mother that. Now that she's the only one left and the land has been passed on to her, she's reluctant to part with it. Her father, grandfather and great-grandfather all insisted there was oil, and according to Mom they were always right about everything else, so why not this?"

She grinned. "It's hard to understand unless you come from generations of prairie people. In the old days their intuition was pretty much all they had to rely on, and some of them got a mite stubborn."

"Just a mite," Tom groaned. "It seems to have been bred into their bones! I've handled other transactions in that general location, but no one else has mentioned oil. The other owners seemed happy to take what they could get for their land."

Carol frowned. "You mean someone is buying up real estate out there?"

Maybe her mother wasn't so far off base after all. Sandhills property was mostly mile after mile of low rolling hills of sandy soil not good for anything but growing hay and grazing cattle. Bringing in irrigation may have increased its value a little, but not much. Was it possible there was oil under the land after all?

"No, no," Tom hastily assured her. "Nothing like that, but one or two pieces have been sold since I've been here."

"How many exactly? One or two?"

He shifted uncomfortably. "Uh...three, to be exact."

Three pieces of property in the same area as her
mother's land changing hands in less than a year
sounded like more than coincidence. Carol decided to
approach the subject from a different direction.
"Tom, I don't believe you ever mentioned who your
buyer is? Is it someone from around here?"

He shook his head. "No, it's a corporation, Long-
acre & Associates, in Kansas City."

Carol's eyes widened. "But why would a corporation in Kansas City want to buy undeveloped property in the Sandhills of Nebraska?"

Tom shrugged. "Honey, as the new kid in town I
don't ask questions. I just take the business and am
happy to get it."

"Yes, of course," Carol murmured. She knew how
difficult it was to start up a new business in a small
town, especially if you weren't a native. "Was Long-
acre & Associates the buyer in the other transactions,
too?"

"Oh, no, there was no connection among those
sales. Each parcel was sold to a different buyer at a
different time. Your mother's wrong. There's no oil
out there—someone would have found it before this if
there were. I wish I could talk to her personally. You
said she wasn't well?"

"She has rheumatoid arthritis," Carol reminded
him. "Mom's not young. She was forty when I was
born, which makes her sixty-eight now, and she's more
or less disabled. She couldn't possibly make the long
trip back here. Even if she flew to Omaha, she'd have
to travel two hundred and fifty miles by car over rough
roads to get to Raindance—it would be excruciating.
No, you'll have to deal with me."

Tom leaned forward and looked her in the eye. "I'll be happy to deal with you, but someone has to make her realize that she's paying taxes every year on a piece of prairie that is darn near worthless. She may never get another offer like this one."

Carol clutched her purse and stood. "The taxes are minimal, but I'll tell her. I'm going to call her tonight. Can we get together again tomorrow?"

He stood also. "Sure. I'm showing a summer cabin over on the Niobrara River in the morning. Would two o'clock be all right with you?"

Carol agreed and left, but on her short drive back to the motel her thoughts tumbled and turned. Why would an out-of-state corporation want her mother's land? And how come there'd been so much activity in Sandhills real estate in the past year?

The situation was more complicated than she'd expected, and she wasn't informed enough to handle it by herself. She'd been away too long. The man she was dealing with was a stranger to her, and she knew nothing about current real estate values in the area. She needed help, but she didn't know whom she could trust. Once, everyone in town had been her friend or a friend of the family, but she'd left Raindance as an outcast. She didn't know who, if anyone, had forgiven her, and she wasn't anxious to find out.

Carol had been innocent of the charges leveled against her eight years ago—she'd even been cleared officially—but most of the townspeople thought Bryce and her parents had bought her freedom with either money or pressure applied in appropriate places. The community had sympathized with Bryce because they'd seen him as a victim, but her moral, pillar-of-the-community parents had capitulated under the censure and had given up everything to leave town six months after Carol had.

She frowned as she swung her car into her parking spot at the Inn. She was in no mood to ask for help or favors.

Back in her room she again reached for the phone directory. Was Norris French still practicing law? He'd been the lawyer for the bank where her father had been president, and the two men had grown up together. Norris had handled her parents' personal legal work. In fact he'd been the one who'd gotten all charges against Carol dismissed, but in doing so he'd made it plain that he considered her a spoiled brat who never thought of anyone but herself.

Well, he'd been right, but by the time she'd faced that fact the damage had been done. At age twenty her life had lain in shambles at her feet.

Norris French, Law, was still listed in the directory, and Carol dialed the number. A pleasant female voice answered. "Law office, may I help you?"

"I'd like to speak to Mr. French, please," Carol said.

"I'm sorry, but Mr. French is on vacation. Would you like to talk to his partner?"

Darn! Norris hadn't even had a partner when Carol had known him. Still, it might work to her advantage. Maybe the partner was someone from out of town who wouldn't know her past.

She told the woman yes, and a few seconds later a husky male voice answered. "Hello?"

The nape of her neck prickled and her whole body tightened. The voice sounded familiar, but who was it? She wished she'd asked the receptionist for the partner's name before she'd agreed to speak to him.

She took a steadying breath. "Hello. This is Carol Murphy from Los Angeles. I'm in town on business, and I need some legal advice."

There was a long pause at the other end, and she was just wondering if they'd been disconnected when the husky voice spoke again: "Hello, Carol, this is Bryce."

Chapter Two

The words vibrated in Carol's brain, and she slowly
sank down to sit on the edge of the bed. *Dear God, it
was Bryce.* No wonder she'd had such a strange reaction when she'd heard his voice—her heart remembered even though she'd carefully erased the sound of
it from her mind.

"B-Bryce?" She didn't recognize the thin, raspy
tone that issued from her throat.

"Carol? Are you all right?"

No, she wasn't all right. She'd known their paths
would cross while she was here—there was no way she
could avoid it in a community this small—but not on
the first day. She needed to get the feel of the town
first, to find out if the antagonism toward her had
mellowed with the years or if it was as strong as ever.
She wasn't ready. She couldn't face him and the scorn
that had seared her the last time she'd seen him.

She should never have come back!

"Carol? Dammit, say something. What's the matter?" There was nothing thin or raspy about Bryce's voice.

She took a deep breath and forced herself to speak. "I—I'm okay. I just wa-wasn't expecting... That is, I was calling Norris."

"Norris is on vacation."

Her fingers clutched the phone so tightly that her knuckles were white. "I know. The receptionist said I should talk with his partner."

"That's me. What do you want?"

He sounded so cold and abrupt, as if talking to her were distasteful to him. Well, it probably was. He'd had no reason to change his mind about her in the years since he'd turned her out of his house and out of his life.

What little composure she had left was disintegrating fast. She couldn't ask him for help. Never! Besides, he was an accountant, not a lawyer. How on earth had he become Norris French's partner?

"I...n-nothing. I'm sorry I disturbed you." She put the receiver back in the cradle, kicked off her beige pumps and curled up in a ball on the bed.

"Carol. Carol!" Bryce swore lustily and slammed the receiver down. She'd hung up on him!

He pushed his chair back with enough force to send it crashing against the wall and, jamming his fists in his pockets, walked across the room to look out the window that fronted on Main Street.

Calm down, Garrett, he told himself. *You got over this woman a long time ago, remember? You knew she was coming back. There are no secrets in small towns, so what's your problem?*

Problem? He had no problem with Carol Garrett . . . Carol *Murphy* . . . anymore. She'd been out of his life for eight years, and no one knew better than he that he was well rid of her. For the two years of their ill-advised marriage she'd kept him hovering in a purgatory between ecstasy and despair until he was almost glad when the whole thing blew up.

Almost. Hell, he *was* glad. Of course, there'd been a period of shock and mourning; but once that was over he'd been happy, content with his new life, his new profession . . . his chilling loneliness.

He shook his head as if to clear it. So why did just the sound of her voice on the phone make him break out in a sweat in his newly air-conditioned office? Why did his heart pound? Damn, how could the mere thought of her arouse this unbidden, aching desire?

Carol lay curled up on the bed for a long time, willing her heartbeat and her breathing to return to normal. But her heart continued to pound, her breath to catch painfully in her chest.

This wasn't at all the way it was supposed to be. She'd prepared herself so carefully for her first meeting with her ex-husband. She'd planned to be calm and cool and sophisticated; the new Carol Murphy. She'd intended to show him that the emotional, self-centered little hoyden he'd been married to had burned herself out, and a well-educated, self-controlled woman had risen phoenixlike from the ashes.

Instead she'd fallen apart the moment she'd heard his voice. She hadn't even seen him; she'd come unglued right through the telephone wires. Good Lord, what must he think?

If only she'd had some warning. In all her preparations, she'd never anticipated surprise. She'd assumed they'd meet face-to-face and that she'd at least see him coming soon enough to pull herself together before she had to talk to him.

After a while, Carol became aware of increased activity outside the motel—cars parking in the spaces in front of the long row of rooms, and people walking and talking and slamming doors. She looked at her watch and was surprised to see it was almost six o'clock. A rumble in her stomach reminded her that she hadn't eaten since she'd stopped in North Platte that morning for breakfast.

She swung her feet onto the floor and sat on the edge of the bed. From there she looked into the mirror on the wall behind the chest of drawers and made a face at her image. She looked like a waif, her eyes red from long hours of driving, her hair disarrayed and coming loose from the fancy braid and her dress wrinkled.

She reached up and unbraided her hair, letting it fall to her shoulders in kinky curls. It looked more disheveled than it had before.

She'd just pushed herself to a standing position when there was a knock at her door. Who could that be? she wondered. No one knew she was here. Then she remembered Scooter—Frank. Maybe he'd dropped by to visit—and try to find out why she'd suddenly come back after such a long absence.

The knock sounded again, louder this time. "Just a minute," she called, and padded in her stocking feet across the room. She'd find some excuse to get rid of him quickly but politely.

Carol pulled the self-locking door open and stared. Standing in front of her like a ghost out of the past was the only man she'd ever loved, the one man who would never again love her in return: her ex-husband, Bryce Garrett.

She blinked, but the image didn't dissolve; it still wavered before her disbelieving eyes. And it was definitely Bryce, dressed in tan slacks and a brown linen sport coat, his blond hair darker now but still golden. He was heavier at thirty-three than he'd been at twenty-five, but it was muscle that padded his six-foot frame, not flab. Maturity had added a completeness to his handsome features and a strength to his bearing. He was a man any woman would be proud to call hers, but a quick glance at his left hand revealed no wedding band on his finger. Of course that didn't necessarily mean he wasn't married.

"May I come in, Carol?" he asked into the long, shocked silence.

"Oh, yes, of course." Thank heavens her voice sounded fairly normal. She stood back to allow him to enter.

As Carol shut the door she turned—and almost bumped into Bryce. He was standing just inches away. He stepped back quickly, and she managed to catch her breath.

"Please, sit down," she said, indicating the only chair in the room.

"In a minute," he answered. "Are you all right? You sounded so odd on the phone, and then you hung up without telling me why you'd called."

His gaze took in her face and hair. "You look—"

Bryce clamped his mouth shut before he could utter the words that lingered on his lips. Carol looked like a child who had been wakened from a sound sleep, all warm and deep and drowsy. He turned away so she wouldn't see the wave of longing that swept through him—a need to cuddle her in his arms and brush the moist tendrils of ebony hair from her pale cheeks.

What in hell was the matter with him? He was reacting like the gullible twenty-one-year-old he'd been when he'd come home from college to find that the little Murphy girl down the street had grown into a seductive young woman in his absence. He'd let his raging untamed hormones rule his better sense then, and it had been disastrous.

Never again, he reminded himself firmly. This woman was poison.

"I'm fine," Carol said to his back as he walked across the room and sat in the chair she'd indicated. "I just . . . well, I wasn't prepared to talk to you when you answered the phone in Norris's office." She moved to the bed and sat down on the edge. "It's been a long time, Bryce," she said, dismayed at the quiver in her tone that she couldn't control.

"Yes." The one word was blunt.

She tried again. "How did you know where I was staying?"

"My, how quickly you forget life in a small town." His tone was sarcastic. "There are only two motels in the area, and somehow I didn't think you'd want people remembering your past connection with The Travelers Rest."

Carol cringed as the painful memory of the rundown collection of one-room cabins across the railroad tracks to the south of town stabbed her. With it came the unwelcome image of Joel Everett that she had carefully buried deep in her subconscious, and her features twisted with anguish.

Bryce's shoulders slumped, and he ran his fingers through his hair. "I'm sorry," he said, and there was genuine remorse in his tone. "That was a low blow. I don't want to quarrel with you. I came to ask what sort of legal advice you need."

"But you're an accountant. . . ."

He shook his head. "I'm also a lawyer. I left town, too, eight years ago—after your parents moved to California. I went back to school and got a law degree, then came back here and went to work for Norris. I've been his partner for over a year now. I assure you I'm no more anxious to take you on as a client than you are to have me for an attorney, but unfortunately we're the only law firm in town. Until he gets back, which won't be for two more weeks, I'm the only choice you have."

The guilt that had tormented Carol for so long came rushing back full force. So Bryce had been driven away by her actions, too. How could someone who would never deliberately hurt anyone have totally disrupted four people's lives the way she had? Hers and Bryce's, her mother's and father's—not to mention those of her aunt and uncle in L.A., who'd taken her in when she had no place to go.

"Oh, Bryce, I'd be proud to have you represent me in anything, but I wouldn't ask that of you. Surely there must be a lawyer in Valentine. It's only fifty miles; I could drive up there and talk to someone."

Bryce straightened. "Fred Hardesty's still practicing there, but if it's only advice you need it's silly to drive all that way to ask a few questions." He glanced at his watch. "I've got to get home, but if you don't mind waking up early, I can see you at seven-thirty tomorrow morning in my office. You can at least tell me what the problem is."

He stood, and she did, too. "Thank you," she said with a smile, determined to maintain what composure she'd been able to muster. "I really appreciate you making the time for me. I'll be there."

He hardly looked at her as he strode to the door and opened it. She followed him, still in her stocking feet.

He was outside when she stopped him. "Bryce?"

He looked over his shoulder. "Yes."

She twisted her fingers together. "Are you married?"

He turned slowly and looked at her through cold, narrowed eyes. "No, are you?"

The relief that flooded over her was overwhelming. "No." It was little more than a whisper.

He didn't respond, but turned again and walked away.

Carol got up at five the next morning and, dressed in white shorts, T-shirt and running shoes, went jogging. It seemed like ages since she'd used her legs for anything but pushing the accelerator and brake pedals of her car, and her muscles responded gratefully to the exercise.

Starting across the street from her motel, she jogged the four long blocks south to the "new" hospital. It had been under construction when she'd left but was now a rectangular two-story building with landscaping in front and parking spaces on both sides. Across the street on what used to be a bare lot was another rectangular building, a medical clinic, bearing the names of two doctors she didn't know.

She turned the corner to the west and continued past the three-building school complex where she'd attended elementary, junior high and high school; three blocks of old homes, neat but in various stages of disrepair; and the big old white house that had been converted into a funeral parlor. Again she turned, this time north, and ran back to the highway where the final turn took her past various apartments, businesses and a senior citizens' retirement complex until, out of breath and dripping with perspiration, she was once more in front of the Raindance Inn.

By the time she'd showered and dressed in a lightweight mauve shantung suit, Carol noticed that the restaurant next door was open, and she headed over to get some breakfast. After Bryce had left the evening before she'd been too drained to change her clothes and go out to dinner. Instead, she'd driven to the locally owned drive-in that was a teen hangout and ordered a hamburger and cola to take back to her room.

Stan's Steak and Stein was nearly empty so early in the morning, but unfortunately the waitress was a woman Carol had gone to school with. Although they'd never been close friends, Vicky greeted her as though they had. Carol tried to respond warmly to Vicky's gushy greeting, but as she placed her order she wondered at the other woman's sudden friendliness.

"So, what ya doin' back here, Carol? Never thought you'd set foot in this town again," Vicky said with characteristic lack of tact.

Carol winced. "I'll only be here a couple of days. I had some business to attend to.

"Seen Bryce yet?"

"I didn't come to see Bryce," Carol murmured, poking at scrambled eggs that had suddenly lost their appeal.

"Yeah, well, you're sure lookin' great." She sounded more resentful than complimentary. "You always could fall into the manure pile an' come up smellin' like a rose. Got a rich boyfriend out there in lotusland?"

Carol bit back a rude retort and stood up. She fumbled in her purse and put some bills on the table beside her half-eaten breakfast. "I *work* in California, Vicky," she said frostily to the astonished waitress, "and that's only baby powder you smell, not rose."

She walked out with her head held high—her dignity intact, but her knees wobbly with the rush of anger, frustration and guilt Vicky's implications had provoked.

Back in her room she took several deep calming breaths, then touched up her lipstick and made sure her French braid was neat and becoming. She was especially anxious to make a favorable impression on Bryce today after he'd seen her at her worst yesterday. Checking the hem of her slender skirt in the mirror, she smiled. He'd always been partial to mauve, or any shade of lilac, on her.

Maybe seeing her looking like a successful businesswoman would make him realize that she'd finally grown up.

Bryce stood at the window of his office facing Main Street and silently cursed himself. He'd gotten here half an hour early for his appointment with Carol, and that told him something he didn't want to know. She still had the ability to get under his skin.

He should have kept her waiting a few minutes instead of being the one to lose sleep and waste time. The office was never opened before eight, but since he'd already had a busy day scheduled he'd offered to open up early to work her in. In retrospect he thought it was a mistake—he shouldn't be giving her preferential treatment. But on the other hand, the quicker she completed her business here, the sooner she'd leave.

The street outside was nearly deserted. Only the bakery in the next block, which had a few tables and served coffee, was open; several cars were parked in front of it, and a few people wandered in and out.

He was tempted to go down and buy some of the fragrant, mouth-watering pastries that were so popular with the townspeople. He hadn't slept well and had finally gotten up at five-thirty. To kill time he'd fixed himself a big breakfast, but had found himself unable to eat most of it. That hauntingly sensuous ex-wife of his had killed his appetite as well as shredded his nerves, and the knowledge made him furious.

Just then a fire-engine red, late-model Jaguar pulled up in front of the building and parked behind his new Thunderbird. Must be a tourist, he thought; nobody in town had the kind of money it took to buy that kind of high-powered foreign bomb. It was sure a beauty, though—sleek and shiny and impressive. It even had windows tinted so dark you couldn't see inside.

As he watched, the door opened and a woman got out. She had her back to him, but even so he knew she wasn't anyone from around here. Her confident bearing, expensive clothes and elegant braided hairdo were those of a city woman, sophisticated and well cared for.

As she shut the door and walked to the end of the car, he saw her in profile and stiffened. No. It couldn't be!

The woman rounded the car and headed toward the building where he stood looking out. He muttered an obscenity as his stomach knotted in pain. It was Carol. And evidently she wasn't above compromising her morals to get what she wanted. The Carol Murphy Garrett he knew had neither the education nor the inclination for hard work required to earn the kind of wages it took to buy a car like that.

Her classy life-style must be subsidized by someone, and it sure as hell wasn't that good-for-nothing Joel Everett. No, this time she'd found a rich patsy. She'd said she wasn't married, so...

He heard the outside door open into the small reception room and suddenly wished he'd asked Lila to come in early. He needed a buffer—somebody to keep Carol away until he could get his temper under control. But it was too late now.

He didn't go to the door of his office to greet her politely but called from where he stood at the window, "Come in here, Carol."

Carol jumped as Bryce's voice shattered the silence of the empty reception room. For a moment she'd thought there was no one around. She strode quickly to the door on her right from which his voice had emanated. No one sat behind the large oak desk, but the room was clean and uncluttered. How like Bryce. He'd always been the one who'd picked things up and put them away—her things as well as his.

Her eyes swept the room, then stopped. He was standing by the window watching her, and she smiled, a bubble of happiness rising within her at the sight of him. "Good morning. Isn't it a beautiful day?"

She walked across the room to stand beside him, and it was only then that she noticed the hard set of his chiseled features. "I should imagine your days are always beautiful," he said coldly.

Carol's blue eyes widened. The words could have been an endearment, but she'd heard the snarl in his tone.

"I-I'm not sure how to take that," she stammered.

"I merely meant that anyone who drives a new Jaguar and wears designer clothes can't have to worry about paying bills. Apparently you finally found a man who can afford to keep you in the style to which you always wanted to become accustomed."

The battering words struck Carol in the solar plexus, and she instinctively clutched her arm across her midriff. First Vicky and now Bryce. Vicky didn't matter, but she'd been stupid to think she and Bryce could ever have any kind of relationship, even a professional one.

He was too bitter—and with good reason, she had to admit, even after all this time. She could understand his rage, but she wasn't going to let him abuse her.

She took a breath and squared her shoulders—and wasn't surprised at the torment she saw in Bryce's wide, cocoa-colored eyes when she met his gaze. Bryce was essentially a gentle, kind man, the sort who comforted crying children and helped confused elderly ladies. It was only she who brought out this side of him, and she tried to remind herself that his lashing out was a response to the pain she'd once inflicted.

He was still hurting, and so was she. He'd loved her once, and she was paying the price for abusing that love, but after all these years surely she'd done her penance. She'd been wrong to come back. The kindest thing she could do for both of them was to leave town again as quickly as possible.

She angled her head and met his gaze unflinchingly. "You are the only man other than my father who ever paid my bills, and no man will ever do it again." Her voice was calm and very low. "I have an M.A. from UCLA and a well-paying job with the public relations department of one of the big television studios. I work hard and probably make as much in a year as you do, and although it's none of your business, I'll tell you how I happen to be driving a Jaguar."

She stopped for breath, and Bryce, looking stunned, shook his head. "No. Please. I'm sorry—"

"I bought it from a well-known actor, who shall remain nameless," she continued as though he hadn't spoken. "The man's a lush and a compulsive gambler, and when his TV series was canceled in midseason he couldn't make payments on the car. He needed cash to pay some of his more pressing gambling debts, so he sold me the Jag for just what he had in it: fifteen thousand dollars. I took five out of my savings and borrowed the rest from the credit union."

She opened her purse and took out her keys, all the time praying that her voice wouldn't break until she'd finished what she had to say. "Now, if you'll excuse me, I'll conclude my business with Trent Realty as quickly as possible and be out of town as soon as I can. I'm sorry I troubled you."

Turning on her heel, she walked away from him and out of the building.

By the time she got back to the motel Carol's whole body was trembling, and when she'd made it to her room, she leaned against the locked door, covered her face with her hands and gave in to the sobs that could no longer be held back.

By early afternoon Carol had regained control of herself, and after repairing her ravaged face with expertly applied makeup, she again looked the part of the successful young businesswoman. It was probably wasted effort, since she'd noticed that most of the women on the street wore slacks, shorts or cotton sundresses, but it couldn't hurt. And if she was going to have to handle this sale without legal advice she needed all the advantages she could muster.

At exactly two o'clock she walked into Thomas Trent Realty and greeted Donna Trent in the reception room. "Hi, yourself," Donna replied, and glanced at the old-fashioned clock on the wall. "You're right on time. Tom and Bryce are waiting for you in Tom's office. You can go on in."

Carol stopped. "Bryce?"

Donna nodded without looking up from the typewriter. "Yeah. He got here a little early. Said he was meeting you."

Carol's first thought was to turn and run. She couldn't survive another scene with Bryce. What could he possibly want? Surely he understood that she no longer expected him to advise her.

She forced her feet to move in the direction of the office and pushed the door open. Tom sat behind the desk, and Bryce occupied one of two chairs in front of it. His back was to her, but he turned and stood when Tom did. "Ah, Carol," Tom said, "you're refreshingly prompt. I've just been filling Bryce, here, in on the offer we've made for your mother's land."

Carol looked from one man to the other. Tom had a big smile, but Bryce's expression was strained and uncertain. "That's right," he said, as if she knew exactly what he was talking about. "Since our meeting this morning...uh...broke up...before we'd had a chance to fully discuss the situation, I called Tom and asked if I could come a little early so he could explain it to me."

Carol blinked. Apparently he was telling her that he'd help her after all, but how had he known she had an appointment with Tom at two? Well, she was still in need of a legal opinion. She wasn't going to be stubborn about accepting his help.

"Thank you. I appreciate it," she said, and sat down in the chair beside him.

The two men also seated themselves, and Tom picked up the conversation. "Now, let's see, where were we? Oh, yes...

For the next hour the two men did most of the talking, with Bryce asking questions and Tom answering them. Rather he attempted to answer them, but Bryce's keen mind picked up inconsistencies and hesitations that Carol wouldn't have noticed, and Tom seemed genuinely uninformed about his client's intentions.

"Damn it all, Bryce," Tom finally said in exasperation, "I'm only handling a real estate transaction for this company, not investigating them. They came to me with a reasonable offer for Anna Murphy's land.

I figured it was none of my business what they planned to do with it."

Bryce's expression softened and he relaxed back in his chair. "You're right. The property's always been considered pretty much worthless, but if Anna has questions, they'll have to be answered. That property's been in the family for generations, and I suspect it has sentimental value."

Carol grinned. "That's true, it does. When I was growing up, every time Mom and her two sisters got together they hassled over Great-Grandpa's estate and badgered Uncle Orrin, who was administrator. They were always sure he wasn't doing it right."

She turned to look at Bryce. "Remember that first Thanksgiving after we were married when we all got together at Uncle Orrin's and—"

Her words skidded to a halt, and a hot flush of humiliation washed over her. Dear God, how could she have been so insensitive as to reminisce about their marriage? And in front of a business acquaintance of Bryce's.

Her mouth snapped shut, and she clenched her hands together in her lap as she lowered her head to hide her flaming face. "I-I'm sorry," she whispered.

Bryce reached over and covered her entwined hands with one of his. It was warm and strong—and heartbreakingly familiar. "I remember," he said gently. "The three women gave poor old Orrin such a bad time about the way he'd handled the taxes that he stormed away from his own table and refused to finish eating."

He squeezed her hands, then removed his and led the conversation around to a different topic.

He'd covered for her. Helped her out of an embarrassing situation. But she suddenly felt she could have handled it more easily if he'd lashed out at her as he had that morning. His kindness was almost more than she could bear. The gentle side of him was the man she'd known and married—the man she still loved, she admitted as her insides twisted in anguish.

She took a tissue from her purse and tried to be unobtrusive as she wiped away the tear that rolled down her cheek..

After a few minutes Bryce pushed his chair back and stood. "I think Carol and I should go out and inspect the property before she makes a decision about selling it. Tomorrow's Friday.... How about if we get back to you on Monday—say, around eleven?"

Monday. But she'd hoped to be able to leave long before then!

Carol stood also and said goodbye to Tom and then Donna as they left the office. Outside, on the street, she turned to Bryce. "Look, I really appreciate your help, but I've decided to advise Mom to go ahead and sell. I imagine we can make some sort of deal to keep the oil rights if that's really what's bothering her. I-I'd hoped to leave by Saturday at the latest."

He took her arm and led her in the opposite direction from her car. "Come back to the office with me and we'll talk about it."

The Norris French law firm was across the street in the middle of the next block. When they got there the rooms were empty, which puzzled Carol. "Don't you have a secretary?" she asked.

"Sure, you remember Lila Upton. She's worked for Norris for over twenty years. I asked her to cancel my appointments for this afternoon and then take the rest of the day off.''

"But why?''

"I wanted to be free to spend as much time with you as necessary.'' He put his hand under her chin and tipped her face up. "You've been crying.''

His touch, and the concern in his voice, made her heart pound. "Not really,'' she said uncertainly. "I was just upset by my blunder in reminiscing—''

He shook his head. "Before that. You'd been crying before you got to Tom's office. I saw it in your eyes.''

Carol started and pulled away from his touch. She'd put cold compresses on her eyes before she'd started skillfully applying makeup. Anyone would have had to study her closely to find telltale evidence of her tears, and it seemed to her that Bryce had barely looked at her when she'd arrived.

He came up behind her and cupped her slender shoulders with his hands, causing her to catch her breath. "Carol, I'm sorry about the way I behaved this morning.'' His voice was unsteady, and his hands tightened. "I acted like a real bastard. I had no right to jump to conclusions.''

Involuntarily her head tilted back slightly to rest against his cheek. "It's understandable. You trusted me once and I betrayed that trust—but not the way you think. I was never unfaithful to you, Bryce.''

He stiffened, and his fingers clenched her shoulders painfully. "It's not important anymore whether you were or not,'' he said harshly. "All that was another lifetime ago. Even if you were living with someone now, it's none of my business. I didn't mean to hurt you.''

Before she could say anything he released her and walked away. "No, dammit, that's not true." His voice was gravelly with emotion. "To my everlasting shame I *did* want to hurt you. I wanted you to feel some of the pain that was gnawing at me. Having you back in town again is...difficult."

Well, at least he was honest. She could be no less. "I know. It's difficult for me, too. I didn't want to come. I fought against it, but there was no way Mom could travel, and trying to do business by mail and phone is almost impossible. When she gets upset it aggravates her arthritis, so I really had no choice."

"Why didn't Emmet handle it? I know he's getting on in age, but—"

"Dad died three years ago, Bryce."

He turned and looked at her. "Oh God, I'm sorry. I didn't know."

"There's no reason why you would. It was his heart. He just went to sleep one night and never woke up. How are your parents?"

"They're fine. Dad was pretty teed off when I gave up accounting and went to law school, but he was proud when I graduated."

Carol smiled gently. "Of course he was. I'm proud of you, too, and I don't even have the right."

A stab of emotion twisted his features, and again he turned from her. "That would have meant a hell of a lot more to me if you'd said it occasionally while we were married." His tone was bitter.

There wasn't anything she could say to that. It was true. She'd been too young and self-centered to realize he wasn't infallible or impervious to self-doubt— that he'd needed her support and understanding as much as she'd ever needed his. And still he'd loved her until that awful night....

"This is not only destructive, but it's getting us nowhere," Carol said, and turned toward the door. "I'll go back to the motel and call Mother for authorization. She'll sell if I assure her there's nothing wrong with the offer. Then I can clear things up with Tom Trent and maybe leave sometime tomorrow."

She started across the room, but Bryce's voice stopped her. "I'm not sure the offer *is* entirely fair. I agree with you that all these recent sales of Sandhills property are suspicious. I doubt if there's oil there, but something's going on. My advice is to wait until we've inspected the area before you tell her to sell."

He went over to his desk and picked up an appointment book. "Let's see, I'm scheduled heavily for tomorrow because I'll have to work in some of the clients I canceled today. The office isn't open on Saturdays, though. I could pick you up about ten, and we could take our time and check out the property—possibly talk to some of the ranchers."

Carol wasn't sure why he was willing to put himself through this, but she owed it to her mother to find out all she could. She nodded without turning around. "All right. If you're sure I'm not putting you out. I'll see you Saturday."

She took another step, but again he stopped her. "Carol." His voice was soft. "Thanks for being proud of me."

Her muscles seemed to melt, and a low moan escaped around the lump in her throat. She turned then and looked directly at him through misty eyes. "Oh,

Bryce, don't you know? I've always been proud of you. I just didn't know you needed to hear it."

Her voice broke on a sob, and she turned quickly and fled.

Chapter Three

Carol slept late the next morning. The long trip combined with the turbulent emotions of the past few days had finally caught up with her, and it was nearly ten o'clock before she woke.

The temperature in the room was comfortable, but a glance out the window warned her that it was too warm for jogging. Unlike California where the heat peaked in the late afternoon and then cooled off, Nebraska weather remained hot but reached a crescendo between noon and one o'clock. The bright sunshine beat against the pavement, and visible waves of heat shimmered in its brightness.

Although it was too sultry for running, if she dressed properly and stayed in the shade, walking shouldn't be a problem. She decided to skip breakfast and take a walk around her old neighborhood. She didn't want another confrontation with Vicky at the restaurant, anyway.

A few minutes later, wearing red shorts and a red-and-white striped loose-knit shirt, she headed west along the highway for five blocks. Reaching Cedar Street, she turned north and slowed her pace.

This was the area in which she'd grown up. At that time the tree-lined streets with their large middle-class homes and well-kept yards were where the town leaders, professional people and businessmen lived. It was still a prestigious area, but by the time she'd graduated from high school several of these families were selling their homes and buying in a newly opened subdivision farther north. Bryce's parents had been one of the first to move, and her own father, president of one of the two banks, was planning to have a house built out there when his only daughter's scandalous behavior had caused him to retire and move away.

Although her parents had accepted her explanation of the unfortunate events and had come to her defense with both emotional and legal support, Carol felt they'd never really believed that she hadn't been cheating on Bryce with Joel Everett. She sighed and looked up from her reverie.

She'd been walking slowly, sifting through the old memories, and hadn't realized she'd arrived in front of the brown shingled house with the glassed-in porch and familiar old cottonwood tree at the side on whose sturdy branches she'd once had a swing. It was the house where she'd been raised, and the sight of it brought a lump to her throat.

Who lived there now? she wondered. Her parents had listed it with Charlie Innis's realty company when they'd moved to California six months after she'd moved out there, and she'd never known who bought it. There was no swing under the tree, nor any other sign of children, but that wasn't too surprising. The house had only two bedrooms, plus her father's den. Her mother had been thirty-nine and her father forty-four when they'd married, and they hadn't anticipated having a family. She'd come along as a surprise, albeit a welcome one. Once they'd gotten over the shock, they'd spoiled her rotten.

She felt a stinging sensation on her bare arm and slapped at the large insect that had lighted there. She'd forgotten about the mosquitoes and the flies. They were a constant problem in the humid summers—not bad if you were in motion, but the moment you stopped they zoomed in and attacked.

She hit at another one, this time on her leg, and she knew she'd have to move on. A third insect buzzed around her head, and she struck out at it just as a car pulled up to the curb beside her and sounded its horn.

She leaned down and looked in the window. It was Bryce.

She opened the door, and his gaze roamed over her bare arms and legs as he ordered, "Get in before you're eaten alive."

She climbed inside and slammed the door. "Gee, I'd forgotten about those bloodsuckers," she said. "I don't even have any insect repellent."

Bryce didn't put the car in gear but left the motor running. "What are you doing here? Were you looking for the Johansons? Marge and the kids spend the summers at their cabin over on the Niobrara River, and Sven commutes."

"No, I didn't even know who lived here," Carol said as she ran her hand over the soft gray leather upholstery. "I just wanted to see the place again. I—I was happy here." She swallowed and changed the subject. "When you drove here I was just thinking that whoever bought it must not have children since it doesn't have many bedrooms."

Bryce grinned. "They didn't when they acquired it—they were newlyweds. But not surprisingly their family has enlarged over the years. They now have two boys and are looking for a bigger place."

Carol looked away, unable to return his grin. She remembered all too keenly how badly he'd wanted a baby and how willfully she'd refused. "I'm only nineteen, for heaven's sake," she'd said. "I'm not ready to tie myself down yet. There's plenty of time for kids later."

Well, she'd been wrong about that. A year later Bryce had filed for divorce. Now she'd give anything to have his children, but she was sure that was the furthest thing from his mind.

She glanced hastily across at him looking so very handsome dressed in slacks and a crisp shirt that was open at the neck and had the sleeves turned back to his elbows. Carol wondered if he really was as heart-breakingly attractive as she thought, or if he just affected her that way because she knew firsthand how it felt to be in his arms—the warmth and gentle strength of his hands as they cupped her breasts or caressed her thighs, the firm but tender pressure of his mouth as it roamed freely over her sensitized flesh, seeking...and finding...and driving her over the edge....

Her fantasizing was interrupted with a jolt when he spoke. "If you'd like to go inside I could probably arrange it with Sven. I'm sure he'd give you a tour."

"Oh no, no, it wouldn't be the same. I was just . . . reminiscing."

Thank heaven he didn't know what she'd been reminiscing about. She felt the flush that she was sure colored her face, and her body throbbed with unbidden and unwanted desire. She was going to have to keep her errant thoughts under control!

Again she noted his glance directed at her long shapely legs, and her blush deepened as her body responded. "You'd better wear slacks and long sleeves when you're outside," he said, his tone murky as he looked quickly away from her. "Those mosquitoes leave big welts that itch."

"So I found out," she said, scratching at a bite rising on her arm. "What are you doing over this way?"

He reached out and turned off the engine. "I'm headed for my parents' house. Mother called to tell me that the mailman left an important overnight express letter I've been waiting for at their house instead of at my office." His tone was heavy with exasperation.

"The mailman responsible wouldn't be the infamous Walter, would it?"

"You remember him?"

She grinned. "How could I forget? Remember the time he messed up and sent your income tax return check back to the IRS with a notation that you were no longer at that address? We needed that money desperately, and it took months to get it back."

He chuckled. "We'd already charged a new sofa against it, and we ate so many hot dogs and hamburgers while paying for it out of my overextended salary that I still can't stomach them."

The merriment fled from his face as quickly as it had come. "Is everything really going okay with you now, Carol? You never seemed to know the value of money. I would have paid you spousal support if you'd requested it, but Norris wouldn't allow me to offer it. At the time I was in such a confused state, I just let him handle things, following his best judgment."

She was surprised. It had never occurred to her that Bryce might have considered supporting her with alimony. Not that she would have asked for it.

"I'm doing fine," she said, anxious to allay any fears he may have for her. "I lived, board and room free, first with Aunt Kate and Uncle John and then with Mom and Dad, and I worked to pay my college expenses. Believe me, I learned the value of a dollar. I worked as a waitress during my undergraduate years. The wages were minimal, but the tips were good. When I went back for my master's the school got me a part-time job with the television company and an offer of full-time employment when I earned my degree. I've been with them ever since. I'm now an assistant manager."

Bryce was genuinely interested to hear what had happened to Carol in the intervening years since their divorce, but still he was distracted by her legs resting so close to his own. She'd lost weight, and it seemed to him that she'd grown a little. She'd only been eighteen when he married her, and she'd still carried a little baby fat. Not that he'd minded—she'd been soft and cuddly and incredibly sexy in his arms.

He dragged his gaze away from her. If they sat here much longer in the close confinement of the car, he was going to make a pass at her—put his itching hands on her bare flesh and see if she would still respond to him as quickly as she used to. And if she did he'd be lost. He never had been able to resist her, and he was appalled to discover that nothing had changed in all those years. But that didn't mean he had to act on his overcharged male urges.

He reached out to turn the key, and the motor roared to life. He'd learned all about hell once because of her; he wasn't going to set himself up for a repeat trip. He finally had his life on an even keel again, and he intended to keep it that way.

Carol was in essence telling him she'd changed completely in the years since he'd last seen her, but he wasn't buying it. She'd grown up a lot—he'd give her credit for that—but she'd been too thoroughly spoiled, first by her parents and then by him, to ever become the kind of woman he needed. His life was falling into place at last, and he didn't intend to shake it up because his body remembered what it should have forgotten long ago: the touch of her hands caressing him, the sound of her throaty voice whispering endearments, and her long legs entwined with his as they rocketed to oblivion and beyond.

He closed his eyes and shivered.

Carol waited for Bryce to comment on what she'd been saying, but his mind seemed to be elsewhere and she wasn't even sure he'd heard her. He'd turned on the engine, and now she realized it was probably his way of telling her he was ready to leave. She opened the door on her side. That seemed to get his attention. "Where are you going?" he asked, looking startled.

"Well, I-I'm sure you're anxious to get your letter and go back to work...."

"Shut the door, and I'll drive you back to your motel."

She turned and slid out of the car, then turned again and bent to look inside. "Thanks, but I want to explore the old neighborhood. The mosquitoes aren't bad as long as I keep moving."

He nodded. "Okay, if that's what you want. Don't forget, I'll pick you up at ten tomorrow. I'll bring along sandwiches and iced tea since there's nothing out there but rolling hills and pasture land."

Carol began walking again as he drove off. Her next stop was in front of the green house on the corner where Bryce had grown up. He had a sister and brother who were considerably older than he, and she'd never really known them. It was Bryce, the "older man" of fifteen, that she'd had a crush on since the age of ten.

He'd tolerated her childish adoration and sometimes let her follow him around when he wasn't with the other guys, but it wasn't until she was sixteen that he really began to notice her. By then he was away at college, but he'd dated her a few times that summer.

The following spring he had graduated from the university in Lincoln and come home for good. They'd started going steady, were engaged by Christmas and were married in June, two weeks after she graduated from high school.

Her eyes settled briefly on the porch swing where they'd sometimes sat, but the mosquitoes began their attack again, and she moved on.

By noon Carol was hungry. She'd strolled past the homes of several of her girlhood friends, had even encountered the mothers of two of them in their front yards and stopped to visit. In each instance it had been pleasant. Both women had greeted her politely and seemed content to let the old gossip lie as they brought her up-to-date on their families and asked about hers.

In all it had been an enjoyable morning, and Carol lost some of her apprehension and felt more at home with each positive encounter.

She considered going downtown for lunch. Yesterday when driving down Main Street she'd noticed a couple of small restaurants, but reluctantly she discarded the idea. She didn't want to appear in the main business district in her abbreviated shorts.

Other women, and most of the girls, dressed that way for shopping, but Carol couldn't forget that she had a tarnished reputation to live down. It shouldn't matter to her—she'd only be here for a few more days and would probably never come back. But it did. Her roots were here. Most of these people had known her since she was born, and she wasn't going to do anything to reinforce their bad opinion of her. At least some of them seemed willing to give her the benefit of the doubt, so when she appeared on Main Street she would wear either a chic dress or tailored slacks and a blouse.

She walked back to the Raindance Inn and changed from her shorts to a skirt, then went next door to Stan's Steak and Stein.

To her chagrin Vicky's shift included lunch, and Carol couldn't think of a polite way to tell the hostess she didn't want to be seated at one of the waitress's tables. She wasn't surprised when that's exactly what happened.

Vicky appeared with her order pad and a cheery greeting that was unsettling. She acted as though Carol had never gotten snippy with her. "So, how are you enjoying your visit?"

Relieved that Vicky evidently hadn't taken offense last time, Carol told her about her walk that morning to the old home neighborhood. She carefully edited out any mention of Bryce. "The town doesn't seem to have changed much, except for a few new businesses. And, of course, the old hospital's been torn down."

"Yeah," Vicky agreed, "we gain a few and lose a few. Have ya been out to the golf course yet?"

Carol looked up in surprise. "Don't tell me Raindance finally built a golf course! My dad and several of the other businessmen tried for years to get the town to put one in, but the budget never seemed to stretch that far."

Vicky laughed, a loud gusty sound that filled the room. "Well, we wouldn't have it yet if old Doc Keller hadn't died and willed the land to the town for just that purpose. It's nice. I don't play golf, but they got a clubhouse that's a beaut. During the week they just serve lunches and snacks, but on Friday, Saturday and Sunday nights they have a buffet dinner that's outstanding."

She lowered her voice and leaned closer. "Why don't ya try it tonight? Their food's a whole lot better'n we serve here. Just don't tell anybody I told ya. I could get fired."

Carol couldn't imagine why Vicky would risk her job to tell someone who'd never been a close friend about a better place to eat, but Carol thanked her and ordered the fresh garden salad.

"Ya want low-cal French or Ranch-Style dressing?"

"Ranch, please, and I'll have a piece of that homemade coconut cream pie later."

Vicky made a face. "I shoulda known you could eat anything without havin' to worry about your weight." Her teasing tone carried an edge of envy. "Oh, and

about the clubhouse. It's called the Eagle's Nest, and
if ya go around seven ya shouldn't have to wait long to
be seated.''

During the afternoon Carol found a Laundromat
and laundered the meager supply of clothes she'd
brought with her. She was glad the yellow linen dress
was washable, because she wanted to wear it that evening.

She'd decided to take Vicky's advice and go out to
the Eagle's Nest for dinner. She knew her mother
would want to know all about it, and the only way
Carol could describe it to her was to go there and see
for herself.

She sighed as she thought of her mother. Her parents had uprooted themselves and changed their entire life-style because, after their cherished daughter
had disgraced herself and them, they'd felt they could
no longer live in the small community where they had
been business and social leaders as well as pillars of the
church. They'd moved to Los Angeles to be close to
Carol, but they'd never again been as happy and content as they had been in Raindance.

The crushing weight of guilt Carol had been carrying around for eight years once again descended on
her. She knew her parents weren't blameless. From the
day Carol was born they'd treated her as if she were a
fairy princess. Old enough to be her grandparents,
they'd centered their lives around her every whim. The
thought of saying no to her or punishing her for dis-
obedience had never occurred to them.

Her upbringing had contributed to her downfall,
certainly, but still she had mostly herself to blame.
There had been other, positive, influences in her young

life. Church, school, scouting, friends and a sprin-
kling of relatives had touched her in ways that might
have balanced her parents' indulgence if she'd been
willing to admit that just possibly the world didn't re-
volve around her.

Unfortunately she'd been strong-willed, stubborn
and absolutely certain that anything Carol wanted,
Carol should have. By the age of twenty she'd had it
all, and before she was twenty-one she'd lost it in one
blinding explosion that hit the Omaha and Lincoln
newspapers and made her name a household word in
Raindance.

By six-thirty Carol had showered and dressed and
was applying the sky-blue mascara and apricot lipstick that was her only makeup for the evening. She'd
shampooed and blow-dried her hair and let it fall in
soft curls around her shoulders.

The golf course was several miles north of town on
a narrow county road. Carol remembered it as the area
where the high-school kids used to park and neck.
She'd done her share of making out under the big old
trees, but never anything serious. Even a dozen years
ago nice girls didn't go "all the way" in rural Nebraska. They kissed and hugged and teased a little, but
they'd really been pretty innocent. Carol hadn't even
let Bryce make love to her until they were married, although she'd gone far enough with him to severely test
their willpower.

She sighed. Maybe the only reason he'd married her
was to get her in bed and finally relieve his frustration. At least in that she hadn't disappointed him.
Their lovemaking had always been fantastic—hot,
urgent and deeply satisfying.

She dragged her thoughts back to the present just in time to turn off the bumpy road onto an even smaller one called Fairway Lane. Hardly original, but it led to the parking lot in front of the new, modern, glass-and-brick clubhouse.

There were quite a few cars in the lot, and she saw several couples coming and going. She felt out of place as a single. In California she almost never went to a restaurant by herself; she either cooked her own meals, picked up fast food and took it home or went out with friends. She hadn't minded Stan's Steak and Stein, since it was on the highway and catered to tourists, but this was a more formal arrangement.

For a moment she debated whether to leave, but decided she was being silly. After driving all the way out here she might as well have a decent dinner, she thought determinedly. She got out of the car and strolled through the parking lot and up the walkway to the heavy glass front door. As she reached for it a feminine voice behind her called, "Carol? Carol Garrett?"

Carol turned around and was delighted to see blond, petite Rosemarie Smith, who had been one of her closest friends. "Rosie," she gasped, and the two women embraced with all the glee of teenagers.

When they'd calmed down Rosemarie introduced the husky man escorting her. "You remember Jim. He's my husband now, and we have two sons. We got married as soon as I graduated from college."

Carol certainly did remember Jim Perkins. He and Rosemarie had been high-school sweethearts, and she and Bryce had double-dated with them often.

Carol would have hugged Jim, too, but he quickly put out his hand, and Carol knew that he hadn't forgotten or forgiven her treatment of his friend Bryce.

As they walked across the lounge the two women talked excitedly. "I heard you were here, but I didn't know where you were staying," Rosemarie said. "Will you be around long?"

"Only a few days," Carol answered, and explained about the real estate transaction.

"Oh, what a shame. But we've got to get together before you leave! We're having dinner with a group from Jim's lodge this evening, but how about Sunday after church? We'll have lunch at the house and spend the afternoon catching up."

By this time they'd reached the wide entrance to the dining room. "I'd like that very much, thanks," Carol said, as she stopped to wait for the hostess.

Jim was urging Rosemarie on into the dining room where, presumably, some of their friends were already seated.

"We live in the Webster house across the street from the park," she called over her shoulder.

Carol nodded and watched the couple head toward a large table across the room.

She was impressed by the tasteful decor in shades of green featuring gold linen cloths and hurricane lamps with lighted candles at each table. The light coming in from the windows was still bright, and her view was unobstructed as her gaze wandered toward the buffet counter. To her surprise she saw Vicky from the Steak and Stein sitting at a secluded table with several other people. Carol was sure the other woman saw her, too, but Vicky leaned over quickly, almost as though she didn't want to be seen and didn't show any sign of recognition.

Just then the hostess returned and led Carol across the room in the other direction. She scanned the crowd as she walked, looking for familiar faces when one seemed to jump out at her.

It was Bryce—and sitting next to him was an attractive woman with short chestnut hair and golden eyes flecked with brown. They were holding hands on top of the table, and their heads nearly touched as they talked.

A cold feeling of dread stole over her. This was no casual business dinner. They had the look of lovers passing time until they could escape the crowd.

Carol stopped, for a moment unable to tear her gaze from them. They looked relaxed and happy—content.

All her life she'd heard the old cliché about wishing the floor would open up and swallow a person, but she'd never realized how true it could be until this instant. She'd blundered in here in front of all these people, and probably every one of them knew of her past relationship with Bryce. Should she pretend she didn't see them and stay, or turn and leave as unobtrusively as possible?

It was then that the thought occurred to her. Had she been set up? Even in a small town it was almost too much of a coincidence that she'd come clear out here at exactly the same time her ex-husband and his date were having dinner.

For that matter she'd probably never have heard of the place if Vicky hadn't made a point of telling her about it. Vicky had not only recommended it highly, but she'd told Carol what time to come.

And she was here now with an audience, waiting to watch Carol make a fool of herself again!

The hostess had stopped at a table a few feet away from Bryce's, and Carol nodded her approval as the woman put the menu down and left. She'd leave a tip even though she wasn't staying, but first she had to defuse this little drama.

Her heart hammered with uncertainty as she pasted a big smile on her face and headed toward Bryce. He hadn't seen her yet, but she called from a table away, loud enough for those near to look up. "Bryce, how nice to see you again."

His head jerked up, and the surprise on his face turned to apprehension and then cold harsh warning as he stood. He thought she was going to make a scene. Well, he had a right. That's exactly what the Carol Murphy he married would have done. Now all she wanted was to reassure him as quickly as possible.

She continued toward the table, silently willing him to act as if she were any casual friend. She hoped he'd make the next move and at least introduce her to his date.

Apparently he decided that he wouldn't get nasty if she didn't, and to her relief the warning look was replaced with a smile, although it still didn't reach his eyes. "Carol. You're looking very pretty." There was no enthusiasm behind his words.

He turned toward the woman still sitting in the chair beside him and put his hand deliberately on her slim shoulder. "Sharon, this is Carol. Carol, I'd like you to meet my fiancée, Sharon Davis."

Chapter Four

Carol's eyes widened and her breath caught in her chest. The pain was swift and all-encompassing, and she forced her knees into a rigid stance to keep from swaying.

His fiancée! He'd said he wasn't married, but he hadn't mentioned he was engaged. Not that he was under any obligation to keep her informed of his love life—but it would have been kinder to tell her in the privacy of his office.

It was Sharon Davis who acted first. She put out her hand and smiled. "Hello, Carol. Bryce told me you were in town. I was hoping to meet you. Please, won't you sit down?"

Bryce frowned, and Carol knew that he wanted her to make a polite excuse and leave, but she sat quickly before her shaking legs gave way.

"Thank you," she said, and lowered her voice as Bryce sat down, too. "I'm sorry to break in on you two like this, but I'm afraid I've just walked into a trap that's closed on all three of us."

The smile still lit her face, but there was chagrin in her eyes and desperation in her voice.

Both Bryce and Sharon looked startled, and Carol plunged on, telling them how and why she believed she'd been set up. "If you'll look across the room to that table in the corner you'll see Vicky and several other people," she concluded. "I suspect they're watching us closely."

Bryce and Sharon glanced discreetly in the direction she'd indicated and nodded. "Yes, they're watching," Bryce said.

"Do you two come here fairly often on Fridays?"

"Yes," Sharon said, "nearly every week, and always at about the same time since Bryce doesn't get away from the office before six."

Carol sighed. "It looks to me like Vicky and her friends wanted to see how the three of us would react if we met accidentally in public. She probably expected me to start something. I guess I'm not really surprised. Vicky and I never did get along. She was a year or so younger and was jealous of me because she had a crush on Bryce."

A dull flush spread over his face, and he made a gesture of protest. This time Carol's gentle smile was genuine. "I didn't mean to embarrass you, but you always were the local heartthrob, you know."

Sharon chuckled. "He still is," she said, and covered his hand with her own.

Carol knew she had to get out of there, but before she could move Sharon spoke again. "I understand you and Bryce are going out to look at your mother's property in the Sandhills tomorrow."

Good heavens, she'd forgotten about that. When she'd agreed to it she hadn't known he had a fiancée. "Well, I do want to take a look at the land, but if you and Bryce had something else planned..."

"No, nothing." Sharon said. "Bryce explained that you were anxious to conclude your business."

Carol looked at Bryce for some sign of his feelings in the matter, but his face was expressionless. She looked back at Sharon. "Why don't you come with us?"

Sharon blinked. "Oh, I couldn't do that. I don't interfere in Bryce's law practice."

"But you wouldn't be interfering. There's no reason why you shouldn't come along. It's not confidential or anything."

Sharon looked unconvinced, and Bryce sat back and said nothing. Apparently he was going to leave the matter up to the two women to decide. Damn him, he'd put Carol in an extremely uncomfortable position.

"There's something else you should think about, Sharon," Carol said. "Whether we like it or not, you and Bryce and I seem to be on public display. It would be best if we make it clear we're on friendly terms. Maybe if everyone knows there aren't going to be any fireworks they'll get bored and find someone else to gossip about."

Carol lowered her head and closed her eyes for a moment. "I'm so sorry that my presence in town has been a source of embarrassment and discomfort to you two. It's like a bad soap opera, but unfortunately there's not much entertainment in Raindance. If Bryce and I go wandering off for several hours alone on the prairie, it's probably going to cause a sensation. If you won't go along, maybe we'd better call it off.''

This time Bryce did react. "That's nonsense. I think you're overstating the problem, Carol, but if Sharon would like to come along she's more than welcome.''

He turned to Sharon and smiled. "How about it, honey? I didn't ask you before because I thought we were sort of an unlikely trio, but since we've already been put on exhibit, we might as well make the best of it. Would you mind coming?''

Sharon looked thoughtful for a moment. "No, of course not. I always enjoy a chance to explore the Sandhills.''

Carol pushed back her chair and stood. "Fine. I'll see you in the morning. I've changed my mind about having dinner, so let's all look happy as I say goodbye and leave.''

Her big smile wasn't quite so forced this time. "It's been nice meeting you, Sharon. I hope I haven't ruined your evening.'' She nodded to Bryce who had stood when she did, and, smile still in place, she turned and walked leisurely out of the room.

The shock of learning that Bryce was planning to marry again had badly shaken Carol, and she had trouble going to sleep. But once she did, she slept well and didn't waken until the alarm sounded at seven o'clock. She glanced out the window and frowned. Instead of the hot sunshine of the past few days, the sky was overcast and gray. It looked like rain.

She dressed in the jeans she'd worn for traveling and a long-sleeved sweatshirt to ward off the mosquitoes. The temperature had dropped at least thirty degrees from what it had been, and the clouds were turning darker as she sauntered into Stan's Steak and Stein half an hour later, determined to play out the little drama Vicky had started.

She seated herself at one of Vicky's tables without waiting for the hostess. As Vicky approached, she eyed Carol nervously, probably afraid Carol had recognized her at the Eagle's Nest last night.

Carol greeted her warmly and gave her order. "Did you try the Eagle's Nest last night?" Vicky asked as she wrote the order down.

Carol smiled sweetly. "Sure did, and it really is a classy place, although once I got there I decided I was too tired to stay and eat. But I ran into Bryce and Sharon, and we had a nice chat. It's great to be back and see so many people I used to know."

Vicky looked distinctly disappointed. "Oh? What did you think of Sharon Davis? Kind of a mousy little thing, isn't she?"

Carol fluttered her eyelashes in mock distress. "Not at all. I thought she was charming. In fact she and Bryce and I are going on a picnic out in the Sandhills today. Sure hope it doesn't rain."

"You're what!" Vicky screeched, and dropped her pencil.

"It'll be such fun," Carol continued, ignoring the other woman's confusion. "I have such a short time left here, and I do want to get to know her well. She and Bryce are so in love."

Carol almost choked on the last sentence, but it came out smoothly. Was Bryce in love with Sharon? Of course he must be, or he wouldn't have asked her to marry him. Carol had been over all this in her mind during the wee hours of the night when she couldn't sleep, and she truly wished them happiness. Bryce deserved it after what she'd put him through.

Vicky picked up her pencil and muttered, "Yeah, I guess so," before she headed for the kitchen, the wind definitely gone from her sails.

When Bryce arrived later to get her he was driving a blue pickup, and he was alone. "Where's Sharon?" Carol asked.

"We'll stop for her on the way out of town," he said. "She's staying at Mrs. York's rooming house out on Highway 16."

"Then you're not living together?" Carol could have bit her tongue the moment the words were out.

Bryce glanced at her out of the corner of his eye as he braked for a stop sign. "You're not in California now, Carol. Men and women around here still don't live together until they're married." His tone was heavy with disgust.

She sighed and leaned her head back against the headrest. "I'm sorry. I wasn't implying you were living in sin. I guess you're right, I do come from a different world."

"How many men have you lived with since you left here?"

She cringed at his implication. "I've lost track," she snapped.

Bryce pulled to the curb on the dismal street at the sparsely populated southern outskirts of town and stopped. His hands gripped the top of the steering wheel and he rested his forehead against them. "I'm sorry," he said raggedly. "You seem to bring out the worst in me. But it's not your fault; it's mine. I've wrestled with the old bitterness for so long. I thought

I finally had it under control, but then you came back...."

She could overlook his snide remarks, but she couldn't bear to see him so upset. Without thinking, she reached out and caressed the back of his bent head. "Oh, Bryce, I understand. Truly I do."

Lifting his head, he leaned back, taking her hand in his. He placed her palm against his cheek and held it there. His face felt warm and smooth and so very familiar. She remembered every curve and crevice.

"Do you?" he said. "I doubt it. I don't think you'd have left me if you'd honestly known what it would do to me."

He put his arms around her and drew her against him.

Carol buried her face in his shoulder and lowered her hand to stroke his neck. "I didn't leave you. You left me."

"Did I?" He rubbed his cheek against her silky hair. "I was so torn up I didn't know what I was doing, but there was no future for us after you got involved with Joel Everett."

The man's name was like an obscenity to her ears, but she didn't have a hope of explaining that to Bryce now. She'd tried so hard at the time, but he wouldn't listen—couldn't possibly have believed her. Now it would only drag up memories that were better left buried, without resolving anything. Bryce had a bright new life ahead of him with a mature and loving woman. The last thing he needed was Carol coming back and reopening old wounds.

"No," she said, "there wasn't. It's best for both of us that you sent me away. Now you have Sharon. She'll make you happy."

"Yes, she will," he said, but his arms tightened around her as if denying his words. "Why did you ask her to go with us today?"

"Why didn't you tell me earlier that you were engaged?"

He stiffened, then leaned back and looked at her. "Touché," he said, and brushed his lips against her forehead before he released her and turned the key in the motor.

As they drove away Carol felt chilled—from within. For a moment all her dreams of the past eight years had come true. She'd been in Bryce's arms again. But it had been merely a temporary aberration, a tiny glimpse of heaven that never should have happened and never would again. Neither of them could afford to let it. Bryce wouldn't allow her to interfere with his plans to marry Sharon, and Carol couldn't survive losing him a second time.

A few minutes later they pulled up in front of the two-and-a-half story white frame home set back off the country road that had been Mrs. York's rooming house for as long as Carol could remember. It was a proper establishment for genteel young ladies, mostly teachers, who had no family in the area. The elderly widow had strict rules and enforced them, which occasionally drove one of her more exuberant renters away. Mostly, though, the tenants merely grumbled, secretly pleased that their residence was so quiet and respectable.

Bryce opened the door. "Do you want to come in?"

Carol shook her head. "No, I'll wait here."

He was out of the truck when she called to him. He looked in the window. "Yes?"

She cleared her throat. "Do you still live in our—I mean . . ."

He looked grim. "Yes," he said shortly, "I still live in *our* house. I rented it out while I was in law school and intended to sell it, but when I came back the housing market was depressed so I just moved in again."

He strode away and up the long walkway to the wraparound porch.

Carol was glad he hadn't sold the house. Actually, it wasn't much more than a cottage, but they'd chosen it and decorated it together. They'd done a lot of loving there, as well as a lot of quarreling. She hadn't been able to bring herself to drive by it yet, and she doubted she would. She wasn't a masochist. She wouldn't deliberately expose herself to that much pain.

Sharon was dressed as Carol and Bryce were, in jeans and a sweatshirt. She was slightly built and looked like a young boy in the garb. She wore no makeup but had added a pair of round, shell-rimmed glasses, which complemented her small heart-shaped face without hiding her tawny eyes.

Carol hopped out of the truck to let Sharon slide into the middle beside Bryce. They greeted each other, then Sharon turned to Bryce. "Where'd you get the pickup?"

Bryce helped her into the high cab. "I borrowed it. There may not be roads where we want to go, and we'd never get across the prairie in my Thunderbird."

Carol, who was several inches taller than Sharon, climbed back into the truck before Bryce could offer help, and as they drove away she looked out the window. "Is Mrs. York still alive? She must be in her nineties. She was old when I was growing up."

Sharon laughed. "I think the woman was born old and will live forever. I've been staying there for two years now and I've never heard her first name. I'm not sure she has one. None of the other tenants know it either."

"What brought you here, Sharon, and where are you from?"

"I'm a teacher. I came to teach fifth grade, and I was born and raised in Fairbury."

"That's in the southeastern part of the state, isn't it?"

Sharon nodded. "It's a fairly good-sized town about ten miles from the Kansas border. My parents and two sisters still live there, and usually I go home for the summers, but this year I . . ."

Her voice trailed off, and Carol knew she was embarrassed about what she'd started to say. Sharon Davis was a nice lady. Too many women wouldn't care at all about the ex-wife's feelings. Bryce was a fortunate man to have found her.

Carol took a deep breath and jumped in to relieve her mind. "Of course you didn't want to leave Bryce. When are you two getting married?"

She'd been careful not to ask that question before, because she didn't want to know. The date would haunt her.

"We haven't set a date yet. We have to get our house built first."

"You're building a house?"

Sharon chuckled. "We won't actually be constructing it, but Bryce will do the contracting once we find a suitable lot."

Carol was relieved to hear that Bryce wasn't intending to move Sharon into the house Carol had shared with him. She still thought of it as *their* house. She sighed. But then she still thought of Bryce as *her* husband.

The ride through the Sandhills was bumpy and slow, and it took them nearly an hour to drive the twenty-five miles. By the time they arrived at Anna Murphy's property the sky was black, and a swirling wind had come up.

Bryce swore under his breath. "I hoped we'd drive out of the storm, but instead we've been going toward it. Carol, open that briefcase on the floor beside you and hand me the map that's right on top. I drew it from the information in the papers you gave me. It'll help us identify the boundaries."

She did as he asked, and he calculated for a while, then drove off across the rolling, sandy prairie. They covered the property thoroughly both by truck and on foot, but found nothing to distinguish it from the area around it. It was all barren, treeless and isolated.

Several hours later they ate their picnic lunch in the truck while thunder rolled in the background and an occasional flash of sheet lightning lit the dark sky.

"Bryce," Carol said, "that was the best ham and cheese on rye I ever ate. You can cook for me anytime." The last sentence was spoken jokingly, but he evidently missed the humor.

"I got enough of that when we were marri—" He stopped in midword, apparently just realizing how gruff and accusing he sounded.

The jab hit home, as they all did, and Carol winced but answered calmly. "Yes, you did, didn't you? I'm sorry. I was teasing, but it was in poor taste."

Bryce crumpled his paper cup in his fist, spilling the last of his iced tea. "My God, don't apologize to me," he grated. "I'm the one who's intent on behaving like a jackass."

Sharon looked distressed but remained silent as Bryce started the engine. "We'd better get back to town," he muttered. "This storm is going to open up and be a gullywasher."

They'd driven less than a mile when a crack of thunder shook the earth as a jagged bolt of lightning split the heavens, relieving the swollen black clouds of their burden.

Bryce's prophecy was accurate, and the deluge of rain obscured everything outside the truck, making driving impossible. He pulled to the side of the narrow road and stopped. Another thunderbolt roared as lightning struck nearby, and Sharon cried out and clutched at Bryce.

He gathered her in his arms and spoke softly to her as she cuddled against him with her face buried in his broad chest, while gusts of wind rocked the truck.

Neither of them paid attention to Carol, who was also trembling with fright. She'd forgotten how violent the storms could get in the Midwest, and she'd never before been caught out on the prairie in one.

She wrapped her arms around herself and huddled in the corner of the seat. She wasn't going to let them know how frightened she was. She'd long ago forfeited her right to protection from Bryce. Sharon was his responsibility now.

Carol bit her lip and closed her eyes to hold back the tears that burned in them.

The cloudburst seemed to go on for hours, but the worst of it actually lasted about ten minutes, easing to heavy rain for another twenty before it finally settled down to a steady but manageable drizzle.

When it grew quieter Sharon apologized for her panic. "I know it's silly, but I'm just terrified of thunder and lightning. I always have been."

"It's not silly at all," Carol assured her. "It's a natural fear. I'm more afraid of the wind. Thank goodness we don't have many wind or electrical storms in California." She laughed, but it sounded shaky even to her own ears. "Of course we have an occasional earthquake, so I guess we're never home free where nature's concerned."

Sharon laughed with her, and Bryce started the truck. Unfortunately the trail that served as a road was clay under the sand, and the tires had trouble keeping their traction in the slippery mud.

A few yards farther was a turn-in to a ranch, and once they'd reached it and swung through the open gate, they discovered the private road was topped with gravel. They all breathed a sigh of relief, and Bryce followed the road to a big, old-fashioned ranch house.

He pulled up into the wide driveway and stopped. "This is the Watt family's Flying W ranch. You two wait here while I see if anyone's home."

He got out of the truck, ran up to the house and returned a few minutes later accompanied by a man dressed in faded jeans, a white cotton T-shirt and well-worn boots. Both men carried umbrellas, and Bryce assisted Sharon while the other man came around to help Carol.

The first thing about him that caught her attention was his thick dark hair with undertones of deep, rich red—an unusual color, reminiscent of polished mahogany.

He opened the door and smiled at her as he held the large black umbrella over his head. "Hi, I'm Rusty."

She grinned and made a production of looking at his abundant hair. "Yes, you are, aren't you?"

His smile became a full laugh. "You better watch that gorgeous mane of yours, little lady, or it'll rust in this weather, too." He took her arm. "Come on, I'll share my umbrella with you."

She jumped down, and he put his arm around her as they ran through puddles of water to the house. She could understand why he'd called her "little lady." Compared with him she was. The man was huge! Not fat, but at least six-feet-four-inches of muscle and bone and sinew, with long legs and a broad chest that tapered to a slim waist and hips.

They met Bryce and Sharon on the covered porch, and the men folded the dripping umbrellas and leaned them against the house while the women hurried inside. The wood-paneled living room had a massive stone fireplace and a hardwood floor partially covered with a round hand-braided rug.

Bryce handled the introductions. "Rusty, you've met Sharon." He put his arm around Sharon's waist.

"Sure have," Rusty said, "and it's a real pleasure to welcome you, ma'am."

Bryce turned to look at Carol. "I don't remember whether you knew Carol...." He paused, obviously uncomfortable about introducing her as his ex-wife in front of his fiancée.

Carol saved him the trouble. She put out her hand. "I'm Carol Murphy, and you're Russell Watt. We were never formally introduced, but I remember seeing you around."

Rusty whooped with laughter. "I remember you, too. You were the prettiest and most popular girl in town, even if you were just a kid. I didn't go to school in Raindance, and of course I was older, so our paths never actually crossed."

Carol wrinkled her nose. "I must say, you're well preserved for being so ancient. You even walk without a cane."

His hazel eyes twinkled with amusement. "Watch it, youngster. You go smart-mouthin' me and I'll show you how thirty-four-year-old cowboys keep little girls like you in their place."

He must have seen Bryce's glower because he immediately changed the subject and addressed all of them. "Come and sit down. Can I get you some coffee? I just made a fresh pot."

He headed out of the room, and Bryce and Sharon relaxed together on the oxblood leather sofa while Carol took a wooden rocking chair with needlepoint cushions.

Rusty returned bearing a wooden tray with a coffeepot, cream pitcher, sugar bowl and four ironstone mugs. "You can doctor it up for yourselves," he said as he set the tray on the highly polished free-form redwood-burl coffee table. "Would anyone like a shot of whiskey in theirs?"

The two women declined, but Bryce dropped his sour look and grinned. "I'd love it, but I have to drive home on those miserable roads of yours, and I'll need all my wits about me."

Rusty took a cup of black coffee and sat in a brown leather overstuffed chair. "They're not *my* roads— they belong to the county. If they were ours we'd keep them in a lot better repair. Wait an hour or so, though, and you shouldn't have much trouble. The water soaks right in out here, in all this sandy soil."

He turned his attention back to Carol. "I'd heard you were back. Will you be here long?"

Carol took a sip of hot coffee. "Only a few more days. I had business to take care of, and Bryce is handling the legal end of it. I'm surprised, though, that word of my return reached you all the way out here."

Rusty looked at her indulgently. "Hell, honey, I don't live out here. My dad, mother and two brothers ranch, but I moved to town several years ago. I just came out for a couple of days to help while Dad and Mom are on vacation. I drive a truck for a living."

"Oh, I didn't know. I just assumed…" Carol knew she sounded flustered. And she was. She couldn't imagine why he'd prefer driving a truck to working the family ranch—especially one as big and productive as the Flying W, one of the most profitable ranches in the state.

"That's okay," Rusty said. "It was a natural assumption. My two older brothers and their families have their own homes out here, and they and our dad are working ranchers, but it just wasn't what I wanted."

"Do you have a family?" Somehow the thought hadn't occurred to her before.

There was a twinkle in his eyes as he laughed. "Not me. I'm a confirmed bachelor. Ask Bryce."

Bryce laughed too. "That's right. Every eligible woman in town has tried to rope and tie Red, here, but all they get for their trouble is the pleasure of his company."

Rusty raised both eyebrows. "Oh, they get a little more than that," he said drolly, and all four of them chortled.

After a few minutes Bryce turned serious. "Hey, Russ, maybe you can help me. Have Bud, Jack or your dad noticed any out-of-the-ordinary activity with the land around here?"

He went ahead to explain the nature of Carol's business, and her mother's wariness. "We're out here today looking at Anna's property, but we didn't see signs of anything suspicious going on. Frankly, I'm stumped. Do you have any information about the other sales in the area?"

Rusty wrinkled his wide brow. "Not really. I'd heard about them. Ranchers keep pretty close track of anything like that, but as far as I know nothing's been done with the land since it was sold. Of course some of it's ten or fifteen miles east, but I'll check with Bud and Jack and give you a ring. Dad and Mother are in Germany visiting some shirttail relatives and won't be back for a couple of weeks."

"I'd really appreciate it," Bryce said. "Could you call me at the office before ten-thirty on Monday? Carol and I have an appointment to meet with Tom Trent again at eleven."

Rusty nodded. "No problem."

The rain stopped as suddenly as it had begun, and before long Bryce indicated they'd better be getting back to town. While he helped Sharon into the truck from the driver's side, Rusty walked around to the other side with Carol. "Where are you staying?" he asked.

"At the Raindance Inn."

"Would you mind if I telephone you later this afternoon?"

Carol looked up at him and met his hazel-eyed gaze. "Why no, I'd be pleased." She was speaking the truth. Rusty Watt seemed like a very nice man.

He opened the door and, putting his hands on either side of her waist, lifted her up and into the high cab. They both laughed. "Goodbye, little one," he said. "I'll be talking to you."

He shut the door and stood back as Bryce backed up and turned around.

The road had dried enough that the traction on the big tires held. When they reached the county highway it was blacktop, and the rest of the way into town was without incident except that Bryce seemed quieter than usual.

He took Carol to the motel first, then drove off with Sharon after reminding Carol of their appointment on Monday.

It was only about half an hour later that Rusty called. "There's something I wanted to ask you," he told her, "but I couldn't do it in front of Bryce and Sharon. Carol, I'd like to take you out, but first I have to know. Is there still something between you and Bryce?"

Carol wasn't sure she understood. "Rusty, for heaven's sake, this is the first time I've seen Bryce in eight years." She sounded as indignant as she felt. "He's going to marry Sharon. Just what are you implying?"

"Whoa, honey, I'm not implying anything. I've known Bryce a long time. He used to be my accountant, and now he's my attorney. I'm sorry to bring it up, but I remember all the fuss and bitterness when you and he split. I was surprised to see the three of you together this afternoon, and even more surprised when he sat here looking like he wanted to punch me out the whole time I was talking to you.''

"That's crazy. I hope you're not going to spread that kind of garbage all over town...."

"Hey, calm down. I wouldn't do that. Look, I'm probably handling this all wrong, but I like you. You're a lot of fun. I want to take you to the dance tonight at the Stockmen's Club, but Bryce is my friend. I'm not going to poach on his territory.''

"His territory!" Carol practically screamed with outrage. "You'd better get one thing straight right now, cowboy. I'm not anybody's *territory*!"

She slammed down the receiver and stomped into the bathroom where she peeled off her clothes to the tune of the ringing telephone, then stood under the shower and muttered invectives about chauvinistic men in general and Rusty Watt in particular.

When she turned off the water twenty minutes later the phone was quiet, but by the time she'd put on her robe and dried her hair it had started ringing again. Thinking she'd calmed down enough to give him the tongue-lashing she'd been rehearsing, she answered it.

"Now don't hang up, dammit," Rusty said. "At least give me a chance to apologize. I'm sorry. I admit to being all the nasty things you've no doubt been calling me. I didn't mean to insult you; I was only voicing a cliché that's been around here forever. I'm embarrassed to say that I didn't even think how it sounded.''

Carol analyzed the apology and decided he really was contrite. "Wel-l-l, if you promise never to say anything like that to a woman ever again, I'll forgive you."

"Thank you." He sounded relieved. "I really am sorry, Carol. Give me a chance to prove it by going to the Stockmen's Club with me tonight."

"What kind of club is it?"

He laughed. "It's not a club—it's just an ordinary bar with a dance floor and a live country swing band on Saturday nights. You are familiar with country swing aren't you?"

"A little. I took a class in it as one of my P.E. courses in college. It was fun, although I never had a chance to put what I learned into practice. If you don't mind having to teach me all over again, I'd love to go."

It was true, she thought, she would enjoy going out with Rusty. But it also seemed like a smart move. If he had noticed a spark of electricity between Bryce and her, then possibly others had. If she were seen dancing at the bar with Rusty Watt it would divert their attention.

Rusty wouldn't mind being talked about, but it could cause trouble if Sharon heard Carol's name linked too often with Bryce's.

Chapter Five

The Stockmen's Club occupied the building that had been known as the Tumbleweed Bar and Grill when Carol had lived in Raindance. The country and western music, live and loud, hit Carol and Rusty full force as they walked in. Carol looked around the big rustic room with a bar and numerous tables and chairs at the front. The back had been remodeled and the kitchen taken out to add a good-sized space for dancing.

In spite of the new, fancy name, it was still more a saloon than a lounge. The floor was made of wide bare planks, the walls were windowless and unadorned except for a few colorful beer posters, and the furniture was beat-up pine. The lights were dim in the front but brighter in back for the dancers.

Rusty led Carol to the only empty table next to the dance floor. "Beer okay for you, or do you prefer something else?" he shouted as he pulled out a chair for her.

"Beer's fine," Carol shouted back, and sat down. "Something light."

She watched Rusty walk over to the bar. His jeans fit snugly across his hips and thighs, and she could see the play of muscles with each step. Tonight he was wearing a fancy blue plaid Western-style shirt, a wide handcrafted leather belt with an intricately engraved sterling-silver buckle and snakeskin boots that must have cost a fortune. All topped by a bullrider-style Stetson hat covering his thick mahogany-colored hair. He was not only all male, but absolutely gorgeous.

She smiled as she realized that every other woman in the room was staring at him, too. She only wished she could feel something for him other than an objective appreciation of his masculine perfection. Would her feelings for Bryce always stand between her and any man who took her out?

She shook her head to dislodge the intrusion of her ex-husband into her thoughts.

When she'd asked Rusty earlier what she should wear, he'd said jeans would be fine, and she could see now that he'd been right. Almost all the women wore either jeans or full Western skirts, with loose-fitting cotton blouses and Stetson hats. The men were dressed like Rusty.

Rusty returned with two thick glass mugs topped with white foam that spilled over the sides when he set them down. Rather than try to talk over the noisy music, he and Carol just watched as the couples bent and twirled and pranced to the rhythm of the country beat. It was a rousing piece featuring two guitars, a keyboard and a drum, and the floor shook with the energy of the dancers.

When the song ended Rusty grinned. "How about it, do you remember enough to give it a try?"

Carol took a sip of her beer. "If we can do it slowly. One misstep in that last dance and a person could get trampled to death."

"Now, you know I'm not going to let anyone trample you," he drawled. "I'll swing you right over their heads if they try."

Carol eyed him appreciatively. "You could, too. I'd forgotten they grow men so big back here on the prairie."

Rusty winked. "It's all that prime beef and country air." He pushed back his chair as the music started again. "Come on, we'll do the Texas two-step. It's slow enough for you."

It didn't take Carol long to get the hang of the shuffle, the Texas two-step and the line dance again, and long before the place closed at 2:00 a.m. she was having a marvelous time. Rusty was a buddy to everyone there, and she knew a lot of them. It was too noisy for much conversation, but she danced with a few of the men and got reacquainted with some of the women during trips outside every so often for a breath of fresh air. Everyone was friendly toward her and seemed glad to see her again.

On the way back to the motel Carol leaned against the cool leather upholstery of Rusty's Ford Bronco. She was tired but happy. "I had a wonderful time," she murmured sleepily. "Thank you for asking me."

He reached over and took her hand. "Now I remember why you were always the most popular gal in town when you lived here—aside from the fact that you were the prettiest one for miles in all directions. You have a smile that lights up everything around you, a sense of rhythm that makes you a joy to dance with and a natural talent for making people feel good.''

Carol squeezed his hand. ''And you have a line that probably gets you anything you want.''

''That was no line, honey, but I do have one that guarantees success if you'd like to hear it.'' There was laughter in his tone as he swung into the motel parking lot and parked behind her car.

He turned off the lights and motor and they sat quietly for a moment. Finally he spoke. ''Carol, will you go out with me again tomorrow night? The Eagle's Nest out at the golf course has a dance band every Sunday night during the warmer months. It's the more sedate type of dancing, and I have to admit I seldom go there. Country swing's more my style, but I promise not to polka to the waltz music or tread on your toes.''

It sounded like fun, and she'd had little enough of that in the past eight years. Carol wanted to go with him, but she didn't intend to do more than eat and dance. Did Rusty expect something else? They were both mature adults, and she wasn't going to play childish games with him.

''Rusty, I like you,'' she said, her eyes finding his in the glow from the Inn's outdoor lights. ''I had a great time tonight and I'd like to go to the Eagle's Nest with you tomorrow, but I don't want you to expect more than I'm willing to give. To put it bluntly, I won't go to bed with you.''

Rusty raised a large hand to tilt his cowboy hat back on his head. ''Hell, honey, that's the first time I ever got turned down before I even asked.''

She felt the hot flush of embarrassment. "I'm sorry.
I didn't want you to think...I mean, I just assumed..."

He chuckled. "You assumed right, but I can control my primal urges. I'd be worried if I didn't get
turned on when I'm close to you, but, frankly, you're
dynamite and I don't want to get caught in the explosion. You'll only be here a few more days, and then I'll
probably never see you again, but I'd have to face
Bryce with six-guns at dawn if you and I made love
and he ever found out."

"That—that's not true!" Carol sputtered. "I'm not
his wife anymore."

"Then you better tell him that, because I've had
experience with jealous husbands, and that's what he
was behaving like this afternoon at the ranch."

She sighed. "You're wrong. He doesn't want me.
He doesn't even like me. He's in love with Sharon. The
only reason he's helping me is so I can wind up my
business quickly and leave."

She opened the door and slid out of the luxury four-
wheel-drive vehicle. Rusty got out, too, and walked
her the few steps to her room. "How about it?" he
asked. "Is it on for tomorrow night?"

She nodded. "If you still want to take me."

"You bet I do." He paused. "I guess I should warn
you we'll probably run into Bryce and Sharon. I understand they like that kind of dancing. Is that going
to be a problem for you?"

Carol hesitated. It was, but she wasn't going to let
the hurt of watching her ex-husband and his fiancée
enjoying themselves make a recluse of her while she
was here. She'd known for eight years that Bryce

would never let her in his life again, so she might as well face it and get on with her own.

"What Bryce and Sharon do is none of my business," she said firmly. "What time will you pick me up?"

"I'm going to be working at the ranch tomorrow, so would seven-thirty be okay? The Eagle's Nest has a great buffet. We'll have dinner before the dancing starts."

Touching his finger and thumb to her chin, he tipped her face up. "Good night, honey. Thanks for a memorable evening."

He brushed her lips with his and left.

Carol slept late the next morning, and when she finally got out of bed her legs and thighs were so stiff and sore she could hardly stand. Country swing apparently used muscles she didn't even know she had, and now every one of them was shrieking in agony.

She hobbled to the bathroom and ran the tub full of steaming hot water, then lowered herself into it and soaked until it cooled. When she climbed out she was considerably more limber and less inclined to wince with every step.

She dressed in her shorts and went next door to the restaurant, where she bought a large container of coffee to go and an *Omaha World Herald* and took them back to her room. Rosemarie Perkins had invited her to come over after church for lunch, and the services ended at noon. Deciding one o'clock would be about the right time to arrive, she settled down to read the paper.

At twelve-fifty Carol parked her red Jaguar in front of the stately old Webster house across the street from

City Park where Rosemarie said her family lived now. She hadn't had time to ask Rosemarie what Jim did for a living, but he must be doing all right. She remembered that she and Rosemarie had always been impressed as teenagers with the Webster home. It was a gracious old two-story place with flower gardens, huge elm trees and, inside, the grandest thing of all, a winding staircase.

Carol smiled to herself as she sauntered up the walk. It was overdue for a new paint job, but otherwise looked pretty much the same as it used to. As she rang the bell she wondered if Rosemarie tended the flower gardens now.

The door opened, and Carol was enveloped in her friend's big hug. She returned the embrace and walked into the foyer. "Oh, you look absolutely gorgeous," Rosemarie said. "Purple was always your best color."

Carol was wearing her mauve suit again, and she smiled and murmured her thanks. "You look wonderful, too, Rosie," she replied. "You haven't aged a day."

The statement was part truth and part exaggeration. Although Rosemarie's face was still young, she'd put on enough weight to look a little matronly in her cool two-piece knit dress.

"Well, I don't feel nineteen anymore," Rosemarie said, and her smile had grown thin. "With two hyper preschool boys to chase after, I just feel worn out most of the time."

Carol caught the note of complaint in her tone. "Of course you do," she said soothingly. "Where are they, by the way? And where's Jim?"

The other woman looked stricken. "Oh...um...Jim took Jimmy, the five-year-old, over to visit his parents, and Billy, the two-year-old, is taking his nap. We have the afternoon to ourselves, so we can let down our hair and talk girl-talk all we want.''

Carol could see her friend was upset. Afraid Rosemarie would break into tears if pushed, Carol smiled brightly. ''Good,'' she said. ''Now what's for lunch? I'm starved.''

The meal was ready, and as they ate Carol gave Rosemarie the rundown she asked for on her life in California. ''So, that about brings you up-to-date,'' she concluded. ''I like my job at the television company, and I'm buying my condominium. I wish Mother's health was better, but we found an excellent practical nurse who is free to live in with her so she can stay in her own home.''

She took the last bite of her chocolate mousse. ''Now, it's your turn. How's everything going with you? Not that I have to ask. With a handsome husband, two little boys and your very own dream home, what more could you want?''

''A little freedom would be nice,'' Rosemarie said bitterly, her mouth trembling. ''S-s-some personal space, time away from the kids, a h-husband who wants a companion instead of a b-b-b-brood mare.''

Her voice broke and she dropped her head in her hands.

Carol jumped up and hurried around the table to embrace the sobbing woman. ''Rosie, honey,'' she murmured, then stroked her affectionately and let her cry.

After a few minutes Rosemarie quieted, and Carol helped her up and led her toward the living room. ''Come on,'' she crooned. ''Let's go in here where we can relax and get comfortable, then you can tell me all about it."

They sat down together on the blue velour sofa, and Carol reached for her purse and rummaged in it until she found a handkerchief, which she handed to Rosemarie. While the other woman wiped her tears and blew her nose, Carol went to the bar in the corner of the room and found a bottle of peach brandy. She poured a generous amount into two snifters and went back to her seat on the sofa.

"Here," she said, handing one of the glasses to Rosemarie. "Drink this. It'll make you feel better."

Rosemarie took the glass but didn't look at Carol. "I'm so embarrassed," she muttered.

"Don't be." Carol took a sip from her own glass. "After all, what are friends for if not to provide a shoulder to cry on?"

"But I wasn't there for you when you needed me."

"You were away at college. Besides, there wasn't anything you could have done if you'd been here. It all happened so fast and was over so quickly. I left town less than a week after the charges against me were dropped."

Carol took another swallow of her brandy. "Rosie, did Jim leave this afternoon because he objected to you asking me here?"

Rosemarie turned scarlet. "It's my house, too," she said. "I can invite anyone I want."

Carol put her glass on the coffee table and slid to the edge of the sofa. "I don't want to cause any trouble between you two. I think I'd better leave...."

"No." Rosemarie's hand reached out and clutched Carol's arm. "He's just so damned hardheaded. You'd think he was some kind of saint the way he goes around judging other people. He seems to forget that I was two months pregnant with his baby when we were married.''

Carol sat back again. She was surprised by Rosemarie's confession but certainly not shocked. "That doesn't sound like a very big sin," she teased. "You were in love and had made the commitment to marry. Surely he wasn't upset about it.''

"Upset! He was delighted.'' Rosemarie shifted with agitation. "I think he did it on purpose. He knew I wanted to get a job and be on my own for a while before we got married. I was just getting my degree; I wanted to get some use out of it. I even had a position lined up as an apprentice buyer in one of the big department stores in Lincoln.''

She put her untouched brandy on the table and stood up. "Jim didn't like the idea, and it did have its drawbacks. He was well established with the telephone company here in Raindance, so it meant we would be living more than two hundred miles apart. I wasn't thrilled about that, either, but I wasn't ready to settle down yet.''

She started pacing. "Then, just before graduation, I discovered I was pregnant. Jim had volunteered to take the precautions. He got carried away once and forgot, but I think now that it was deliberate. It sure brought me to heel in a hurry. We were married a short time later, and I was delegated to the role of wife, mother and homemaker.''

The bitterness in her voice grated on Carol. "There are a lot of women who would be delighted to change places with you.''

"Oh yeah? Name one," she challenged.

"Me.''

Rosemarie stiffened with surprise. "You! Oh, come off it, Carol. You've got a glamorous career, your own condo, a fabulous foreign sports car—and I'll bet men fall all over themselves trying to get your attention. Best of all, you can do as you damn well please without worrying about how it will affect someone else."

Carol stood, too, and her tone was sharp. "Yes, I did that once, remember? And I lost everything that gave my life any meaning. What's so great about working until you're so tired you're ready to drop, then going home to an empty apartment and a TV dinner that tastes like sawdust? As for men, most of them want to move in with me so I can support them."

"You're just saying that to make me feel better," Rosemarie said waspishly. "If you were so happy with Bryce then why did you have an affair with another man?"

Carol ran her hands through her hair. "I didn't have an affair with Joel. Not the way you mean. I was never unfaithful to Bryce, but he won't believe that."

She made a gesture of appeal with her hands. "Believe me, Rosemarie, being footloose and fancy-free isn't all that great at our age. In just a little over a year I'll be thirty, and all I've got to show for it is a broken marriage, an education and a few expensive toys. I want a husband whom I love and who will love me. I want children—several of them—and I want to be the one to raise them."

She could see by the skepticism in her friend's face that she wasn't being very convincing. "I don't mean I want to be some man's chattel. But what's so wrong about being a wife to your husband and a full-time mother to your children? Every year I wait makes that dream more unlikely."

Rosemarie turned away impatiently. "You were always a rebel. You never let anyone tell you what to do, but I've been under some man's domination ever since I was born. First my father, now Jim—not to mention two little boys who demand all my attention. I never have any time to myself. I can't even go to the bathroom without a little one toddling along behind me.... And to top it all off I'm pregnant again." She sank down once more on the couch, looking despondent and forlorn.

Carol realized her friend needed counseling, but she also knew she had neither the training nor the time to attempt it. She'd had plenty of experience handling difficult artistic temperaments at the TV studio, but it would take more than the few days she'd be in Raindance to help Rosemarie.

Carol sat down beside the other woman. "Rosie, I strongly suggest you have a talk with your doctor about possible surgery after the baby is born to prevent this from happening again."

"I already have," she said, "but meanwhile it's going to be forever before they're all in school so I can have some breathing space and do what *I* want once in a while."

Carol took Rosemarie's hand. "I know it seems like that now, but you have your education. Once the last child's in school you shouldn't have any trouble getting started in a career of your own. You'll only be in your early thirties. You'll have all the rest of your life to work and enjoy your family, too. A lot of women aren't lucky enough to have both. Like me, for instance. It's scary to look into the future and see no one but yourself."

Rosemarie gave her a wavering smile. "It won't be like that. You'll get everything you want—you always have. But thank you for letting me babble on and for being so understanding. It's helped more than you know."

It was a few minutes past seven-thirty when Rusty knocked on the door to Carol's room and she opened it. He walked inside and stood looking at her, the admiration in his eyes making her feel good all over as he whistled, low but respectfully. "Honey, you're going to be a sensation tonight. I'll have to spend all my time fighting off the men who want to take you away from me. Did you know that blue dress just matches your eyes?"

She did know, and she was glad she'd brought it. She hadn't intended to—hadn't thought she'd need anything so dressy—but at the last minute she'd folded it into the suitcase since it was jersey and wouldn't wrinkle.

"If anyone's going to have to fight off competition it'll be me," she said with a smile. "You look pretty great yourself."

He was wearing Western dress pants and a matching jacket, with a white Western shirt, a bolo tie, boots and his Stetson—a style of dress that was casual but expensive, Carol noted.

When they'd reached the Eagle's Nest Carol was aware they were being watched as they followed the hostess to their table. Once seated, Rusty asked for bourbon on the rocks and Carol ordered white wine. They could hear the orchestra tuning up, and Rusty explained that the dance floor was in the adjoining room that could be glimpsed through the open double doors.

As they enjoyed their drinks several couples stopped by their table to chat. They were people Carol had known when she lived there, and they asked about her parents and her life on the Coast. It was exciting to see old friends again, and Carol was feeling almost giddy as they finished their drinks and headed for the buffet table.

Baron of beef and baked ham were the entrée choices at the buffet, accompanied by assorted cooked vegetables, cold salads and warm dinner rolls. For dessert there was a choice of apple crisp or ice cream. Rusty took both.

The music began while they were still eating. It was the big-band sound, played by a group from Omaha. "The country swing combo that plays at the Stockmen's Club is local," Rusty explained, "but the groups they get here come mostly from Omaha and Lincoln. I believe there's one from Fremont that plays occasionally, and on the fourth of July they always have a big bash and bring in one from Denver."

It wasn't until they'd finished their meal and were threading around tables on their way to the dance hall that they spotted Bryce and Sharon at a table with Jim and Rosemarie Perkins and a couple Carol didn't know.

Both Rusty and Carol saw them at the same time, and his fingers tightened on Carol's arm. "We can't avoid them," he murmured in her ear. "Their table's right in our path. We'll have to stop and at least say hello."

Bryce watched their approach with an expression of cold indifference, but he and the other men stood and greeted them. Rusty, who knew the other couple, introduced Carol simply as "Carol Murphy from California."

Rosemarie looked somewhat abashed. "You didn't tell me you were coming here tonight," she said to Carol.

Carol laughed. "You didn't tell me you were coming, either." She looked at Rosemarie's husband. "Sorry I missed you this afternoon, Jim."

His cheeks turned pink as he muttered something about being sorry, too.

It was Rusty who got them off the hook. "Well, we'll probably see you later, at the dance," he said as he put his arm around Carol to move her on.

The dance hall was a cavernous rectangular room with a bandstand at one end and a candy and refreshment booth at the other. There were two rows of chairs in the refreshment area and an ornamental railing to separate the dancers from the spectators. Rusty paid the entrance fee to the man in a booth to the right of the doors, and they held their hands out to be stamped so they could come and go.

Rusty was as good at conventional dancing as he was at country swing, but he scoffed when Carol told him so. "Aw, I'm pretty much out of practice anymore. I learned when I was in high school, but I prefer the country beat. I'll take guitars over saxophones anytime."

The music started again, and this time it was a waltz. Rusty grinned. "Come to think of it, the orchestra plays more slow music, and that does have its advantages."

To illustrate he put his arm around her waist, and they moved in dreamy rhythm. "Oh yes, this definitely has its advantages," he murmured against her ear as she laid her cheek on his chest.

It was about an hour later, after a rousing rock-and-roll tune, when Carol and Rusty drifted over to the refreshment stand. They were both out of breath. "What'll you have?" Rusty asked when they'd finally pushed their way through the crowd and up to the counter.

"Orange soda," Carol said, and he ordered that and a cola for himself.

They'd moved away from the counter with their drinks and were leaning against the wall catching their breath when Bryce appeared in front of them. "You two enjoying yourselves?" he asked.

"You bet."

"Very much."

They both spoke at once.

"This is a real bonus for the community," Carol continued. "I can remember when the only music we had to dance to was a jukebox or someone's record player. A dance hall with live music must bring in people from all over this part of the state. The place is jammed."

Bryce looked around him. "Yeah, it does. In the two years since it was built it's been a boon to the economy. We don't have all that much new industry coming to town, and the golf course and clubhouse together hire quite a few people."

He looked back at Carol, his gaze intensifying. "I understand you're a country swing enthusiast. You and Rusty didn't lose any time getting together, did you?"

The remark stung, but it also angered her. Obviously he was going to think the worst of her no matter what man she was seen with or why.

Before she could tell Bryce to mind his own business, Rusty did. "Careful, old son." His tone was low and dangerous. "We've been friends a long time, and I value that friendship, but Carol is my date, and it's none of your concern where we go or what we do."

Bryce's fists clenched at his sides. "She's my..."

Wife. The unspoken word hovered in the air.

"Yes?" The tension was thick. "She's your what?"

Just then, almost as if on cue, Sharon walked up to them. "There you are, darling," she said to Bryce as she smiled at Carol and Rusty. "Sorry I took so long, but there was a line in the ladies' room."

The tension was broken, and both men relaxed slightly as the orchestra struck up another piece. Rusty surprised Carol by turning to Sharon and asking her to dance. She looked questioningly at Bryce and he nodded. "I'd love to," she said, and put her hand in Rusty's as they walked over to join the dancers.

This was the last thing Carol had expected. Surely Rusty sensed that she didn't want to be left alone with Bryce.

Before she could regain her balance Bryce took her arm. "Dance with me, Carol." His voice was husky.

Incapable of resisting, she walked with him to the crowded floor. She caught her breath as he put his arm around her waist and took her hand. He'd changed his brand of shaving lotion, but she liked the new scent. It was subtle but intensely masculine. If she wasn't careful, she thought, she'd melt into a puddle right there on the dance floor.

As they moved in time to the upbeat rhythm she was aware of every inch of his body where it pressed against hers, and when his hand at her back dipped to the rise of her buttocks and pushed her closer she missed a step but made no protest.

Bryce was aroused and wasn't attempting to hide it from her. Carol was aroused, too. He had removed his suit coat for dancing, as had all the other men who'd worn them, and her dress was silky but lightweight. She wondered if he could feel the heaviness of her breasts and the hardness of her nipples as they pressed against his thin cotton shirt.

Bryce was an excellent dancer, and Carol found she could follow his intricate steps as easily as she always had. They were so attuned to each other that she knew what he was going to do before he signaled it.

"Rusty apparently decided we needed a few minutes alone together," he said as they circled the room. "He was right."

"Yes, he was," she agreed, "but when we're alone we just say nasty things and hurt each other. I don't want to be hurt anymore, Bryce."

"Neither do I, but the pain is already so intense that I can't help striking out at you. The only other way to relieve it is like this—" his arm around her tightened "—and now that I've got you in my arms again I'm not sure I can let go. That's the worst torment of all," he said, his voice dropping to a husky whisper, "watching you, having you so near, and not being able to touch you."

He was describing her feelings exactly, but before she could tell him so the music stopped. Muttering a curse, he released her but reached for her hand and held it hidden between them until the next piece started.

It was a slow one, and Bryce turned to her and put both arms around her waist. "Hold me," he said softly, a note of pleading in his tone, and Carol clasped her arms around his neck as they danced in place in the darkened corner of the room.

Drawn to his familiar warmth, she snuggled against him, and, with a groan, he lowered his head to lay his cheek against hers. "Carol, you're driving me mad," he murmured. "Are you going to spend the night with Rusty?"

She was too deeply caught up in his spell to take offense. "No. Are you going to spend the night with Sharon?"

As soon as the words were out she wished she hadn't asked. If he was, she didn't want to know about it.

"No." Bryce paused a moment then spoke again. "If I asked you, would you spend the night with me?"

"Yes," she answered without hesitation, "but if you just want a one-night stand to work me out of your system—or for old times' sake—or for revenge—then I'd be saddled with a crushing burden of guilt at having betrayed Sharon. She doesn't deserve it, and I've already got all the guilt I can handle, so please don't do that to me."

His arms tightened around her again, and for a long time he said nothing as they continued to move to the music. Finally he spoke. "You've got a point." His tone betrayed what his words cost him. "Sharon deserves better than that. I expect her to be faithful, and she has the right to expect the same from me. Until you came back I was never tempted to be otherwise.

No one knows better than I the agony of loving someone who cheats on you.''

Carol stiffened and stood still. "Oh, Bryce," she said raggedly, "I never cheated on you, but you don't even listen, do you? I've told you in every way I can think of that I never made love with Joel Everett, but you don't want the truth. You just want to go on punishing me for the rest of my life.''

She turned and dodged dancing couples as she walked off the floor.

Chapter Six

Carol kept going until she'd reached the refuge of the ladies' room, and she hid there until her stomach stopped churning and she was sure she wouldn't break into tears. Then she went out and found Rusty. He took one look at her and spoke gently. "Do you want to leave?"

She nodded. "Please, if you don't mind."

He put her hand through his arm, and they walked to the Bronco in the parking lot.

"You and Bryce have more words?" he asked on the way into town.

She leaned back against the seat and sighed. "He's never going to forgive me. He won't even listen when I try to explain."

"It's a blow to a man's ego, to say nothing of his spirit, to be cuckolded."

Silhouette's

Best Ever 'Get Acquainted" Offer

Look what we'd give to hear from you

Look what we've got for you:

... A FREE compact umbrella set
... plus a sampler set of 4 terrific
Silhouette Romance® novels,
specially selected by our editors.

... PLUS a surprise mystery gift
that will delight you.

All this just for trying our preview service!

With your trial, you'll get SNEAK PREVIEWS
to 6 new Silhouette Romance® novels a month
at $1.95 per book—and FREE home delivery
besides.

Plus There's More!

You'll also get our newsletter, packed with news of your
favorite authors and upcoming books—FREE! And as a
valued reader, we'll be sending you additional free gifts
from time to time—as a token of our appreciation.

THERE IS NO CATCH. You're not required to buy a single book ever. You may cancel preview service privileges
anytime, if you want. The free gifts are yours anyway. It's
a super-sweet deal if ever there was one. Try us and see!

Get 4 FREE full-length Silhouette Romance® novels.

Plus
a handy
compact
umbrella

Plus
a surprise
free gift

▼ PLUS LOTS MORE! MAIL THIS CARD TODAY ▼

Silhouette's Best-Ever "Get Acquainted" Offer

Yes, I'll try the Silhouette preview service under the terms outlined on the opposite page. Send me 4 free Silhouette Romance® novels, a free compact umbrella and a free mystery gift.

215 CIL HAXP

PLACE STICKER
FOR 6 FREE GIFTS
HERE

NAME _____

ADDRESS _____ APT. _____

CITY _____

STATE _____ ZIP CODE _____

Gift offer limited to new subscribers, one per household. Terms and prices subject to change.

Don't forget...

...Return this card today to receive your 4 free books, free compact umbrella and free mystery gift.

...You will receive books before they're available in stores.

...No obligation. Keep only the books you want and cancel anytime.

If offer card is missing, write to: Silhouette Books, 901 Fuhrmann Blvd., P.O. Box 1867, Buffalo, NY 14269-1867

She winced at the ancient crude word. "If he'd only believe me, he'd know that he's suffering needlessly. He called me a cheat, but I never cheated on him."

"It'd help if he could trust you to tell him the truth, but he's still entitled to be bitter. The whole town thought, and with good reason, that you'd been sleeping with another man. He had to endure the taunts and the whispers behind his back and the pity. Whether you were guilty or not, you put him in an impossible position, and he's been living with it for eight years."

Carol closed her eyes. Neither Bryce nor Rusty had touched her with anything but tenderness, but their words left her feeling battered and weary.

"I'm sorry you think badly of me, too, Rusty." She sounded as dejected as she felt. "I like you, and hoped you'd understand."

He reached over and took her hand. "I don't think badly of you, honey. You were barely out of your teens at the time and still headstrong and rebellious. If you'd been my wife I'd have horsewhipped the other man and then taken you home and tamed you down a tad. Damned if I'd have let you get away. But Bryce is a different temperament. He couldn't take the long view, and now he's all tied up in knots because he can't get you out of his system."

They'd reached the Raindance Inn, and Rusty parked in the empty stall next to Carol's Jaguar. He got out of the Bronco and went around to help her down.

He took her key and opened her door, then switched on the light and followed her in. She looked at him as he closed the door, and he grinned. "I just want to say goodbye without everyone who goes past watching. I probably won't see you again. I have to leave tomorrow morning to pick up a load of cattle and truck them to Omaha. I'll be gone several days, so you'll no doubt leave before I get back."

Carol felt as if she were losing an old and dear friend. She'd only known him for two days, but he was friendly, compassionate and a lot of fun to be with.

She put out her hand, and there was a catch in her voice as she said, "I guess this really is goodbye, then."

He ignored her hand and took her in his arms. "I'm afraid so. I wish we'd had more time, but it wouldn't have worked out anyway. You're still crazy in love with your ex-husband."

Carol put her arms around his neck. "Is it that obvious?"

He rubbed his cheek in her hair. "Apparently not to him, but it is to me. Goodbye, Carol Murphy Garrett. I hope someday you'll find the happiness you deserve."

His kiss was warm and tender and loving—and bittersweet with a hint of regret for what could never be. Then he was gone.

Bryce reached over and fumbled with the blaring alarm until he finally got it turned off. Damn, it seemed like he'd barely gone to sleep.

Actually, he had. After tossing and turning and pacing the floor for hours, it had been dawn before he'd finally calmed down enough to drift off. Then he'd slept too hard, and now he had a headache, a natural result of all the whiskey he'd consumed during his nocturnal battle with his libido.

He wanted Carol. Wanted her with a fierceness that gave him no rest. It wasn't something he had any control over. No matter how he tried to deny it, ignore it, drive it out, it burned his loins and twisted his guts and turned him into a bitter cynic who seemed to take delight in taunting her.

He sat on the edge of the bed and rubbed his hands over his face. Delight? There was no feeling of vindication when her features twisted with pain at his angry jabs. At those times he hated himself more than he'd ever hated her, but he couldn't seem to keep from spitting them out.

If she'd fight with him like she used to when they were married it would be easier. Why didn't she defend herself? She'd never before been willing to take criticism, but now she just stood there looking wounded and let him tear into her.

He got up and stumbled out of the bedroom and down the hall to the bathroom. She was coming to the office at ten-thirty. He couldn't stand many more of these confrontations. Regardless of what Rusty found out from his brothers about the sale of property in the Sandhills Bryce was going to recommend that Carol turn the matter over to him and go back to California.

He should have done it before. He'd known all along that he didn't really need her here in order to investigate the sale of her mother's property. He could do that just as well without her. Better, because when she was with him he couldn't keep his mind on what he was supposed to be doing. But every time he'd tried to suggest she leave, he'd come up with an excuse for asking her to stay, instead.

He rubbed shaving foam on his face and picked up his safety razor. His time was running out. He suspected he couldn't face the fact of her leaving him again, but if he didn't send her away, fast, he'd find himself on his knees begging her to stay. That was unthinkable. She'd always been a compulsive flirt, and she hadn't changed. Look how quickly she'd captivated Rusty Watt. Bryce couldn't live with a woman like that, and wouldn't if he could.

He had Sharon now. She was sweet and generous...and bland.

He ran the razor down one side of his face. So what if she was the type who would ration their lovemaking to once a week on Saturday night at ten o'clock? He didn't need passion. He'd had it, and all it had gotten him was two years of mind-blowing pleasure—and eight years of hell. At least Sharon would never be able to hurt him the way Carol had.

He moved the razor to the other cheek. His mind was made up. When Carol came to the office he'd urge her to go back to California as quickly as possible, maybe even later today.

A sharp stinging pain in the vicinity of his cheekbone brought his attention back to his image in the mirror. He'd gouged his face with the razor, and blood was trickling down his cheek like crimson tears.

At exactly ten-thirty that morning Carol opened the door to the law offices and entered the small reception room. A gray-haired matronly woman whom she recognized as Lila Upton, Norris French's long-time secretary, smiled and greeted her pleasantly, then said, "I'm sorry but Bryce is on the phone. He should be finished any minute. Won't you sit down?"

She motioned to a couple of chairs against the wall, then asked about Carol's parents and clucked sorrowfully when told that Emmet Murphy was dead.

The door to one of the inner offices opened and Bryce appeared. "Come on in, Carol," he said, and moved back so she could walk past him.

Bryce looked tired, she thought—she hoped he'd had as much trouble sleeping as she had. His habit of building fires in her, then only partially dousing them with an icy drenching of contempt had made sleep an elusive luxury.

"I've just been on the phone with Rusty's brother Jack," he said after they'd seated themselves on opposite sides of his desk. "You probably know that Rusty's out of town."

She nodded and held her breath, waiting for one of his bitter remarks. It didn't come. "The Watts started checking into the recent sales after we talked to Rusty on Saturday, and they've found that a couple of the smaller ranches have been approached with offers to buy, too. They've scheduled a meeting of all the cattlemen within a hundred-mile radius for Thursday, and Jack wants me there as the Flying W's legal adviser."

Carol didn't know much about real estate, but it all sounded rather strange. "Is Tom Trent handling all the sales? Couldn't we just make him tell us what's going on?"

Bryce shook his head. "No, Tom's as mystified as we are. He's only been involved in yours and two others. The rest are all different realtors. One in Valentine, another in Norfolk and a third in Kearney."

"Kearney? But that's a long way from here."

"Exactly. There's too much secrecy, and all the properties involved either border one another or come close. There are several possibilities, but no one's selling until we get some answers."

Conflicting feelings of hope and despair warred in Carol, but she tried to keep them out of her voice. "Does that mean I'll have to stay here until then?"

Part of her wanted to be near him at any cost, but her more rational self cringed at the emotional devastation of continuing to see him, knowing she could never have him again.

Bryce didn't answer immediately, and it seemed to Carol that he was wrestling too long with a decision that should have been a simple yes or no.

"I suggest that I cancel our appointment with Tom and tell him we need more time," he said finally. "Meanwhile, I'll continue the investigation, meet with the ranchers and talk to some people I know in the capitol."

He absentmindedly reached for a pencil and worried it with his fingers. "As for whether or not I'll need you here..." He was looking across the room, but it was a vacant, unfocused stare. "Yes, Carol, I will." His tone was rough, almost as if the words had been dragged out of him. "I think you should stay in Raindance until this matter is settled, one way or the other."

The pencil snapped in two under the pressure he was exerting on it.

Carol left the office a few minutes later, after Bryce had assured her he'd keep in touch. Now that he'd canceled their appointment with Tom Trent she had the entire day free and nothing to do. Unable to bear the thought of going back to the motel, she decided to reacquaint herself with the business district.

Not that there was much to explore—just four blocks known as Main Street that started at the highway with a gas station on each side and ended with the train station and the railroad tracks, neither of which got much use anymore. In between were office buildings, the post office, Knickerbocker's hardware store, Dillingham's automotive supply shop, several bars, a couple of small coffee shops, Bertoldi's variety store, two banks, Harcourt's department store, three grocery markets and a variety of small shops.

The run-down hotel up the street from the train station, which used to be filled with travelers and railroad workers when the trains ran regularly, now housed senior citizens on small pensions. One building had been torn down, leaving a vacant lot with a board fence across it, and The Beauty Shoppe had become Hester's Hairstyling Salon.

It was in Laura's House of Fashion, one of the little shops, that Carol met Sharon. She'd gone in to browse among the racks of shorts and slacks when Sharon came out of the dressing room carrying a bathing suit. They greeted each other, and Carol eyed the garment. "Shopping for a swimsuit?"

Sharon sighed and returned it to its hanger. "Yes, but they're all so...so *naked*."

Carol laughed. "Oh, come on now, that one must have at least an eighth of a yard of material in it. How much more do you want?"

Sharon didn't join in the teasing, but started looking through the rack again. "That's fine for the beaches in California, but for a teacher to wear a suit that revealing at the swimming pool in Raindance,

Nebraska, would earn her a reprimand from the school board.''

Carol sobered. "You're kidding."

Sharon shook her head. "Would that I were."

"But that's invasion of privacy—and probably illegal. Schoolteachers can't be dictated to like that anymore."

Sharon grimaced. "Well of course they can't," she said with more than a hint of sarcasm, "and we're all modern, broad-minded citizens here in Raindance, but our parents are very protective of their children. Teachers are role models, and as such they're expected to behave in an exemplary fashion. Two years ago I replaced a teacher who didn't. She used to let her boyfriend sleep over once in a while, but they got a little careless about it and there was talk. She was young and didn't have tenure, and the following year her contract wasn't renewed. No reason given."

Carol was incensed. "That's disgusting."

Sharon shrugged. "Depends on whether you're a career woman or a parent. In a town this size you either conform to the moral code or get out. I should think you would understand that, Carol."

Carol was almost overwhelmed by the rush of painful memories that washed over her. "Yes, I should." All the starch had gone out of her. "I guess I'm an incurable optimist. I keep expecting things to change for the better. They can't pull something like that with you, though. Surely you have tenure. Besides, Bryce is an attorney. He wouldn't stand for it."

Sharon turned to look straight at Carol. "That's exactly why I don't flout the town's standards. Bryce has had more than his share of rebellious women. I'd lose my job before I'd put him through something like that again.''

Carol knew she deserved Sharon's scorn, but she hadn't been prepared for it, and it hurt. Up to now they'd had a distant but friendly relationship, and Carol genuinely liked the other woman.

Sharon was just what Bryce needed in a wife—mature, well educated and a lady. She'd give him well-mannered children, keep his home spotless and be a hostess without peer. The only place she might disappoint him was in bed—she seemed a little too inhibited to be the kind of partner Bryce wanted—but Carol couldn't let herself think about that part of their life together.

Carol's distress must have registered on her face, because Sharon reached out to touch her arm. ''I'm sorry,'' she said. ''I didn't mean to be judgmental. The words just slipped out. I'm not immune to feelings of jealousy, you know. I'd be stupid if I were. Actually, I know very little of what happened between you and Bryce, except that he was deeply hurt. I want to spare him any further pain if I can.''

Carol put her hand over Sharon's. ''I know. So do I. I'm glad he has you now, honest, but I admit to being jealous as hell. I wish I'd been more like you.''

Sharon smiled as they both dropped their hands. ''And I wish I were a little more like you. Well, now that that's straightened out, how about having lunch with me? Although breakfast and dinner are included in my rent, I keep sandwich makings and a few electrical appliances in my room for lunches and snacks. We can have some privacy if we go there.''

''I'd love to,'' Carol said, delighted for the company. ''I'll follow you in my car.''

Sharon's room was a large one at the back of the second floor of the old house. It was hot and stuffy when they entered, and Sharon turned on the small air conditioner that was mounted in one of the windows.

Besides the necessary bedroom furniture, Sharon had two comfortably upholstered platform rockers with a small square marble-topped table in between that held a brass lamp. In one corner was a short refrigerator with a Formica top that doubled as a counter. It was a clean, neat room, but Carol couldn't imagine living in it. Her own two-bedroom condo seemed like a palace in comparison.

While Sharon fixed tuna sandwiches, Carol opened a couple of cans of cola, and they ate their lunch at TV tables set up by the rocking chairs. They talked of changes that had taken place in the town, and Sharon brought Carol up-to-date on the local gossip. "...So five months after the wedding they had a 'premature' baby boy who weighed eight pounds, eleven ounces, and was twenty-one inches long. Caused quite a stir around here until something new came along to talk about. The child's about three now, and cute as can be."

Carol leaned back and sighed. "Which, I guess, proves that if you stay and face the disgrace, the town will get used to it after a while and find someone else to gossip about. I suppose that's what I should have done, but I was afraid. I'd hurt too many other people besides myself."

Sharon stirred restlessly. "Carol, I don't mean to pry, and you certainly don't have to talk about it if you don't want to, but would you mind telling me just what happened eight years ago?"

Carol's eyes widened. "You mean you don't know?"

"No, not really. I've heard several versions since I started going out with Bryce, but none of them jibe, and Bryce refuses to talk about it at all."

Carol was amazed that Bryce hadn't taken the opportunity to give his new love the straight story and absolve himself of any blame in the process.

Sharon continued. "I've been told that you were the only child born when your parents were in their forties and that you were badly spoiled. Also, that you were more or less the town darling and won all the school academic and social honors as well as the attention of all the boys.

"Everyone even agrees that you and Bryce were married young and seemed to be the ideal couple. But from then on the story gets scrambled in the telling. I feel it's unfair of me to pick and choose what I want to believe, because of course I'd prefer to think that you were totally at fault for the breakup of your marriage and Bryce was the innocent victim. Unfortunately, it seldom works that way, and I think it's important to my future with him to know what really happened."

Carol was silent for a moment. She didn't want to relive the experience by talking about it. It was still a raw wound to her; but it was equally so for Bryce, and Sharon was right. It was important that she have all the facts. The least Carol could do for Bryce was to tell her so he wouldn't have to.

She ran her fingers through her dark hair. "You're right, all the time I was growing up I'd been led to believe that I was entitled to anything my little heart desired, and I took it, greedily and without appreciation.

The only thing that didn't fall into my lap for the plucking was Bryce.''

Sharon looked startled, and Carol managed a smile. "I adored him from the age of ten. We lived on the same block, but he was five years older and regarded me as that pesky Murphy kid who was always following him around.

"As I grew older my adoration became more sensuous in nature and I began weaving romantic fantasies around him, but he still treated me like the child I was. It wasn't until I was fifteen that he finally noticed I was growing up. He was in college then, but he teased me a lot that summer about becoming a real beauty. He still didn't take me out, though, and I was agonizingly jealous of the girls he did date.''

She could still feel the sharp stab of pain she'd experienced when she'd gone over to his house one evening to borrow something for her mother and found Bryce kissing Lorraine Fairchild in the living room. His parents weren't at home, and in those days no one ever locked their doors. Bryce had yelled at Carol to get lost, and she'd run home, shut herself in her room and cried for hours.

She brought her attention back to the present and continued. "The next summer, when I was sixteen, he finally asked me out. By that time I was considered pretty wild by the adults, although I didn't find out what 'wild' was until I went to California and saw what some of the kids out there were doing. Compared to them I was a model of propriety. I didn't smoke, I only drank beer if I was teased into it and, although I did make out with some of the guys, I never went all the way. I got my reputation by being a party girl. I loved to run with the crowd—dance, go to the movies, whatever. That was more of a high for me than anything I could drink or smoke.

"Bryce and I dated several times before he went back to the university for his senior year, but he wouldn't ask me to go steady and we each went out with others, too. It wasn't until he graduated and came home for good that we got serious. I started my senior year in high school that fall, and we got engaged a few months later. We were married in the spring, and I was supremely happy. I think Bryce was, too—at first."

No, she didn't think, she *knew* Bryce was happy at the beginning of their marriage. They were so much in love and had waited so long for the marriage vows that, once they'd finally managed to escape from the reception, they stopped at the first decent motel they came to on the road to their honeymoon destination of Omaha and spent the rest of the afternoon and the night making love.

Carol felt a stinging sensation in her hands and noticed she'd clenched them so tightly that her nails were digging into her palms. She forced them to relax, then squirmed uncomfortably.

"I don't know how to explain what happened after the first bloom of the honeymoon wore off. I loved Bryce. I never doubted that. Still, by Christmas of that year I was restless and dissatisfied, and so was he. I was a disaster as a wife."

She saw Sharon's gesture of protest, and held up her hand. "No, please, I mean it. I'd never been taught to do the simplest household chores, and I knew nothing about responsibility. I'd somehow managed to exist in a vacuum of self-indulgence for eighteen years, and I actually expected it to continue after I left my overly-permissive parents. I couldn't cook, clean or even do the laundry, and I was insulted that Bryce would expect me to. He began nagging me to clean the place up and feed him once in a while, and I was always after him to take me out in the evenings and on weekends."

Carol's voice began to quiver, and repressed tears stung her eyes. "Believe me, Sharon, even if that had been all that was wrong with our marriage, it would have broken up and it would have been my fault. For a long time Bryce was patient and loving and really tried to teach me how to be the wife he needed. I was totally oblivious to my own faults. I honestly thought all I had to do was keep him happy in bed and everything would work out."

She saw Sharon wince, and wished she'd been more circumspect. No woman wanted to hear about her fiancé's love life with his ex-wife. "I'm sorry," she said, "but that actually was the only thing we had going for us, and after a while it was spoiled, too."

She wasn't going to tell Sharon how badly Bryce had wanted a baby. That would only be painful for both of them, and surely he'd already told Sharon of his hopes for a family.

"Our quarrels became more bitter and more frequent. Bryce was exhausted from working all day and partying with me all night, and the testier he got the more defensive I became. I ran up bills for clothes and nicer furniture but refused to try to get a job to help pay them. I wasn't trained to do anything. When Bryce would get really upset about my indifferent housekeeping I'd run to Mom in tears, and she'd come over and clean for me."

At this point Sharon interrupted. "Now look, I think you're laying it on a little thick. I can't believe that you were as bad as you say you were. It's not necessary for you to take all the blame. I'm sure Bryce was partly responsible."

Carol shook her head sadly. "I wish I could agree with you, but I can't. Bryce put up with me a lot longer than most husbands would have."

She hesitated. She didn't want to go on. Sharon wouldn't insist. She was much more understanding than most women would be in the same circumstances. She wouldn't make Carol walk through that bed of hot coals. Still, she had a right to know the truth and not have to rely on the gossip that was no doubt totally distorted by now.

Carol curled up in the chair with her legs and feet under her. "We'd been married two years when Joel Everett came to town. He was young, handsome and sexy, and every girl and woman in town was interested.

"I met him at a party just a few days after he arrived, and immediately I recognized a kindred spirit: he was unattached, undisciplined and uncaring about anyone's wishes but his own."

It was odd, but Carol could no longer visualize Joel. She couldn't remember the color of his eyes or the shape of his mouth or even the size of his nose. He'd become a faceless phantom who didn't even inhabit her nightmares anymore.

"He was a drifter with plenty of money but no obvious source of income. He stayed at The Travelers Rest motel not far from here and said he was a salesman. He was sometimes gone for several days at a time, but never mentioned what he was selling.

"Being the natural coquette that I was, I couldn't resist flirting with him. I was used to a lot of male attention, and the only kind I'd been getting from Bryce for a few months preceding Joel's arrival was complaints. I wanted to let him know I was still attractive to other men—to make him jealous."

The tuna sandwich Carol had eaten felt like it had turned to stone in her stomach, and the muscles at the back of her neck seemed tied in knots. Suddenly she couldn't sit still any longer, and she got up and went to the window overlooking the back. "I loved Bryce," she said huskily. "I always loved him, and I never for a moment considered going to bed with Joel. I'd always been able to keep the boys I'd dated in line. I didn't even make love with Bryce until our wedding night, but with my usual unconcern I ignored the fact that Joel was neither a boy nor an honorable man intent on protecting me from himself."

She felt her nails digging into her palms again and tried to relax a bit by walking around. "I started meeting Joel for lunch or for an afternoon drink. At first we were discreet, but when Bryce obviously didn't hear about it I began taking more chances. After all, how could he be jealous if he didn't know what was going on? It became an exciting, adolescent game that I was too stupid to realize was dangerous."

She took a deep breath and forced herself to go on. "Then, one night Bryce and I quarreled because he'd promised to take me to a square dance in Bassett but at the last minute had to work late instead. I was furious, and to retaliate I got in touch with Joel and asked him to escort me. Even he argued against it, but I was determined to have my own way and he finally gave in.

"Well, to make a long story short, we went to the dance but left early. Only, instead of taking me home, Joel took me to his cabin. I protested, but he said he just wanted me to have a drink with him. I didn't want to seem unsophisticated so I agreed."

She stopped pacing and leaned against the wall, but she didn't have to close her eyes or search her memory to dredge up the scene that had followed—the small, hot, stuffy room with the unmade bed and dirty clothes strewn on furniture or tossed carelessly on the floor.

"He poured whiskey in two water glasses and gave me one," she said. "I'd never had whiskey before and it burned all the way down, but I drank part of it to prove how grown-up I was. I was sitting on the bed—there were no chairs—and he came over and sat down beside me. I started to get up, but he grabbed my arm and pulled me back down."

Carol could still hear the rough frustration in his tone as he'd snarled, "Oh, no you don't. I've put up with your teasing because it made the final goal even more exciting, but enough's enough."

She leaned more heavily against the wall as she realized she was trembling. "I fought, but he pushed me onto my back on the bed, then ripped my blouse open and rolled partially on me with one of his legs thrown across both of mine. I tried to scream, but he covered my mouth with his and smothered the sound."

Carol put her shaking hand to her lips and looked straight at Sharon. "That's the way Bryce found us seconds later when he opened the unlocked door and stormed in."

Chapter Seven

Sharon gasped. "Oh, my God! But surely you were able to convince Bryce you were being forced. He could see—"

"But there's more," Carol said, so calmly that she had all of Sharon's attention. "Bryce didn't exactly ask for an explanation. He grabbed Joel, jerked him off me and hit him with such force that he knocked him clear across the cabin. Before I could react he'd picked him up and hit him again."

Carol moved her hands to cover her ears as though trying to shut out the memory of the dull popping sound of Bryce's fist against Joel's jaw.

"I yelled at Bryce to stop. I was afraid he'd kill Joel if he kept hitting him. I guess my screams must have penetrated his fog of violence, because he just dropped Joel in a heap and turned to me."

Sharon's eyes widened. "Oh, Lord, he didn't hit you, too?"

Carol shook her head vigorously. "No. He'd never do a thing like that. He just looked at me with the most awful withering contempt and c-called me a s-s-slut."

She pressed her lips together to stop their trembling, then continued. "I tried to tell him what had happened, but he was too enraged to hear what I was saying. He let loose with a blistering diatribe about how I-I was nothing but a t-t-tramp...."

Tears spilled from her eyes and ran down her cheeks as she fought to keep her voice under control. "I knew I was in the wrong, and I was terrified of losing Bryce, but my unbridled temper got the better of me and I yelled back at him. We had a shouting match that must have been heard by that whole end of town, and I-I made the m-m-mistake of threatening to l-leave him."

She wiped at the tears but it was a losing battle. "H-he just looked at me like I was a th-thing instead of a p-person and told me to go ahead, he didn't want me anymore. Then he slammed out of the cabin."

Carol felt Sharon's arms around her before she was aware that the other woman had moved from her chair. "Come back over and sit down," Sharon said. "You don't need to say anymore. I get the picture."

She led Carol, who by now was sobbing, back to the rocker, then moved away and came back a few minutes later with a liqueur glass filled with a beige milky liquid. "Here," she said, and handed it to Carol. "It's Irish cream whiskey. I don't have any of the regular kind, but this might calm you a little."

Carol took it and sipped as Sharon handed her a box of tissues. When Carol had her runaway emotions under control again, she took a long shuddering

breath and settled more comfortably in the chair. "I'm
sorry," she said. "I thought I'd cried all my tears years
ago, but I can't stop the story now. The worst is yet to
come."

Sharon sat down again, too. "I don't need to know
anymore." There was kindness in her tone.

"Yes you do," Carol said. "I won't let you believe
that Bryce sent me away on unreliable evidence. By
that time I was hysterical, and when Joel finally managed to pull himself together his only thought was to
get out of there before Bryce came back and had at
him again. I was too upset to be left alone, and I
couldn't think straight enough to tell him where I
wanted him to take me. I couldn't go home—Bryce
had said he didn't want me. And I was too ashamed to
wake my parents in the middle of the night, so finally
he just started driving out of town.

"I was sobbing and carrying on and not paying any
attention to where we were going until Joel stopped the
car at a rundown farmhouse way out in the sticks. I
protested, but by that time he was furious and snarled
something about the whole mess being my fault and
how I should shut up and come with him. I was more
than a little afraid of him in that mood, and besides I
was only partially aware of what I was doing as he
grabbed my wrist and pulled me along."

It was at this point that Sharon interrupted. "Carol,
you're pale as a ghost. I'm going to insist that you
leave it be. I'm sorry I ever brought it up. I had no idea
this would upset you so."

Carol took another deep breath. "I'll be all right,
and there's not much more. Please let me finish."

Sharon hesitated. "Well, if you insist—but I don't
want you to make yourself sick."

"I'm awfully hazy about what happened next. The whiskey Joel had given me, plus the shock of the scene in the cabin and Bryce's rejection all seemed to run together. I was almost catatonic when Joel shoved me into that house. The place reeked of liquor and smoke, and I recognized the sweetish odor of marijuana. It grows wild around here, and some of the kids I'd run around with in high school smoked it once in a while.

"There were several men and two women sitting around a rickety kitchen table counting money. They started to berate Joel for bringing me there, and he put me in the living room and told me to stay there. I was too traumatized to do anything else. I'd nearly been raped, had witnessed a brutal fight scene between two men over me and had been thrown out by my husband. By then I was little more than a zombie.

"Finally Joel came back with a bottle of whiskey and insisted I drink some of it. I did, and it went straight to my head. I remember going into a bedroom and lying down on a bed. Later I was only vaguely aware that someone crawled in on the other side and immediately started to snore."

Carol's mouth felt dry, and her voice was getting raspy. She cleared her throat. "Could I have a glass of water, please?"

"Of course," Sharon said, and brought it to her.

Carol took a long drink, then held the cool glass against her flushed cheeks as she started talking again. "It was getting light when I woke to the sound of all hell breaking loose.

"Shouts, screams, whistles and the sound of a gunshot brought me upright on the bed, frozen with terror. I thought the world was coming to an end. Bright lights flashed in my face, and someone pulled my hands behind me and snapped handcuffs on them. Before I knew what was happening I was loaded into a van and, with the rest of them, taken to the county jail. We were booked on charges of drug dealing and possession.''

Sharon muttered an oath that was distinctly unladylike. ''But you weren't involved. You didn't even know what was going on!''

The corners of Carol's mouth turned up in a grim little smile. ''Right. That's what I tried to tell the officers, but it was the stuff of which nightmares are made. The first big cocaine bust in the staid, rural, Bible Belt area of Nebraska, and every newspaper in the state carried a picture that had been taken by one of the federal agents of me and Joel, sitting in the middle of the rumpled bed, looking stoned out of our minds.''

''But what happened?'' Sharon sounded outraged. ''Surely they couldn't make the charges stick.''

Carol shrugged. ''I spent the rest of the day in jail and was tested for drugs and found clean before Bryce was able to get me released on bail.''

She shuddered as the image of Bryce's face, white and taut and twisted with pain and shock, rose to haunt her. It was in those few hours that she'd grown up, all at once, and it had been an excruciating experience. It also had been too late to save her marriage and the life she'd known up till then.

''He took me home and told me to pack my things and get out,'' she said in a soft monotone. ''For once I had the good sense not to argue. I went to my parents, who were as outraged as Bryce. They all thought I'd been making love with Joel when we were caught. When the picture was published they were sure of it.''

"But didn't they let you explain?"

"Oh sure, I could explain all I wanted to, but no one believed me. Don't blame them. You wouldn't have either. After all, Bryce had found me in a compromising position on the bed with Joel right after he'd learned what the rest of the town already knew, that I was sneaking around having secret meetings with the handsome traveling salesman. Then just a few hours later I was in bed with him again, but this time in the glare of strobe lights.

"Go to the newspaper office and look up the picture: Joel and me, obviously taken by surprise, my blouse torn, my skirt pulled up from twisting around in my sleep and both of us with that swollen, heavy-eyed look that was actually induced by too much whiskey and the resulting stupor, but could also have been the stamp of a long night of passionate loving."

Sharon looked stunned. "Surely you weren't prosecuted on the drug charge."

"No, Bryce was an accountant then, not a lawyer, but he and my dad hired Norris French and got the charges against me dismissed. It didn't make any difference, though. I'd been branded as a junkie and an adulteress. Everyone figured Dad had somehow bought my freedom. I left town in disgrace, and shortly afterward Dad retired from the bank and he and Mom moved to Los Angeles, too, unable to live with the shame.

"I never saw or talked to Bryce again until now," she said as she again fought back tears. "I ruined my parents' lives, and my own, as well, but I'm glad Bryce managed to survive and find you. Be kind to him, Sharon. I put him through so much hell."

Sharon ran her fingers through her short brown hair and sighed. "Yes, I intend to. Are you happy now, Carol? I understand you've earned a college degree and have an exciting job."

"That's right. My smug little world disintegrated that night. I lost my innocence, or rather my stupidity, and for the first time I had to start being responsible for myself. It was sink or swim, and I discovered that I'm a swimmer. Am I happy? I suppose so. I have a good job with a bright future, and I'm reasonably content."

Sharon looked at her warily. "Are you still in love with Bryce?"

Carol hesitated. Just how honest should she be with Bryce's fiancée? Was it necessary, or even advisable, to bare her soul? After all, the chances of him ever forgiving her and wanting her back were practically nil.

You're backsliding, said the nagging voice of her conscience. *You know what you want, what you intend to do, and if you don't tell her you're no better than you used to be. At least let her know what she's up against.*

Carol took a deep breath and plunged on. "Yes, I'm still in love with him. I always have been and always will be. He's my husband, Sharon, and I want him back."

Sharon stiffened but said nothing. "I never gave him up," Carol told her. "I left him because he wouldn't let me stay, but I never wanted to end the marriage. I admit I shouldn't have come back here, but I did. And now that I've seen him again I know that my love for him is still as deep and strong as ever. I don't think there's one chance in a million he'd ever want to resume our marriage, but if he makes a pass at me I'll respond, and I'll give him anything he wants if there's any possibility he might love me again.''

Carol watched Sharon closely, hating the anguish she was causing the other woman but unable to prevent it. She wasn't going to sneak around behind Sharon's back and try to steal Bryce from her. Neither was she going to walk meekly out of his life again. She'd atoned for her sins, and Bryce still had feelings for her even if he tried to deny them.

"I realize that's not very honorable," she continued, "but I promise you, Sharon, I won't make any moves on him. If he doesn't want me I won't try to seduce him.''

Carol went to bed early that night for want of anything else to do and was up at dawn the following morning, Tuesday. The next two or three days promised to be interminable since she couldn't expect to hear from Bryce again until after the cattlemen's meeting on Thursday. She couldn't face being cooped up in the room. Sharon certainly wouldn't welcome a repeat visit, and she felt uncomfortable contacting Rosemarie again when Jim objected to his wife associating with her.

She couldn't blame Jim. He was Bryce's friend, and Carol knew he wasn't shunning her on moral grounds but because she'd hurt Bryce so badly. She admired him for his loyalty.

She switched on the television to an early morning news show and an idea occurred to her: she'd drive to Omaha. She could be there before noon, and that would give her plenty of time to visit the TV studios there and check in with their public relations departments. She was always intrigued by how other stations handled their PR and never failed to drop in when she was in another city. She could stay the night and be back in Raindance late Wednesday afternoon.

She pulled her suitcase out of the closet and started packing. A few minutes later she stowed it in the car, then walked down to the office to let them know she'd be gone for a couple of days but would be back.

There was nobody at the desk, and after waiting several minutes she finally gave up and left without saying anything.

Omaha had grown and changed in the almost ten years since Carol had last been there. She registered at the Red Lion Inn and luxuriated in the spacious room with thick carpeting, a soft mattress and an upholstered sofa and lounge chair where she could sit in comfort.

She found the phone directory and made calls to set up appointments with the local TV stations, then bathed and dressed in her mauve suit and ate lunch in the coffee shop before setting out for her interviews.

It was nearly nine o'clock Wednesday evening when Carol drove back into Raindance and parked in front of her door at the Inn. She grabbed the handle of the suitcase on the seat beside her and stepped out of the car. The trip to Omaha and her talks with the television PR people had been exciting and productive, and she was glad she hadn't wasted the time moping around Raindance, bored and lonely.

She unlocked her motel room door and had just stepped inside when the door was pushed wide and held open as Bryce's voice grated from behind her, "Where in hell have you been?"

She jumped and stumbled on into the room with Bryce following. "Bryce," she squealed, spinning around to face him. "You scared me. Where did you come from?"

He was standing only inches away and glowering down at her. "I've been sitting in my car waiting for you since I left the office at five," he said angrily, glancing down at the luggage still in her hand. "Where have you been for the past two days and who were you with?"

Carol's eyes widened with surprise and she set the suitcase on the floor. "I've been to Omaha, and I wasn't with anybody. Bryce, what's the matter with you? There was nothing for me to do here, so I drove to Omaha to visit the TV studios and see how their public relations departments are run. It was a business trip."

For a moment he just looked at her, then he slumped sideways against the wall and rubbed his face with his hands. "Oh," he said. The anger was gone, replaced by what sounded to Carol like relief. "I was afraid...I mean, I thought...that is, when your car was gone and no one seemed to know where you were I suspected you might have decided to go back to California after all."

Was it possible that the idea of her leaving town had upset him this badly? Her heart pounded as she stepped closer and reached up to brush a lock of blond hair off his forehead. His skin was hot and damp, and deep lines slashed his haggard face. Her hand slid down to cup his bristly cheek. "I wouldn't go back to California without telling you, Bryce," she said softly. "I've never run away from you."

A ragged moan seemed torn from him. "Don't touch me, Carol," he implored, then negated the request by putting his own hand over hers and holding it more closely against his face. "Why didn't you leave word where you were going? Frank, the manager, said you hadn't checked out, but the maid told him most of your things were gone."

She rubbed her thumb across his mouth, and he kissed it, sending shivers down her spine. "I'm sorry. It never occurred to me that you would worry—or even know I was gone. I did go to the office to tell them I'd be away for a while, but it was so early when I left that there was no one there."

He put his arms around her waist and she put hers around his neck and nestled her head in the hollow of his shoulder. He was trembling, and in an effort to soothe him she snuggled closer and kissed his shoulder through the thin cotton of his shirt.

His arms tightened, and his voice was hoarse as he spoke. "I've been worrying about you ever since I was five years old, and your parents brought you home from the hospital all pink and white and soft. What makes you think I can stop now?"

"I'm truly sorry, darling. . . ." The endearment just slipped out, but she meant it sincerely. In her thoughts he would always be her darling husband. "The last thing I want is to cause you more grief."

For a long time they stood holding each other. Carol could feel Bryce's heart thumping against her breast in a comforting, steady beat—faster than she'd remembered, but then, her heart had sped up, too. Surely he could hear it hammering away in a duet with his own.

Finally he broke the silence. "I'll probably be in that meeting with the ranchers most of the day tomorrow, but I'll need to talk to you afterward." His voice was raspy. His hold on her hadn't loosened, and he caressed her ear with his lips as he spoke. "I'll pick you up here around seven and we'll have dinner."

Just the thought of having dinner alone with him made her blood race, but she was no longer the spoiled child concerned only with her own wants. She raised her head to look at him. "Sharon, too?"

His expressive brown eyes narrowed. "No." It was short and abrupt.

She wanted so badly to forget about Sharon, to take whatever crumbs Bryce would toss at her and let the other woman worry about herself. But she couldn't. The least she could do was spare Sharon the agony of knowing the town was gossiping about her fiancé and his ex-wife. "Bryce, there's no place we could go alone together that we wouldn't be seen and gossiped about, even though it's only a business dinner meeting."

"Yes there is," he said. "Trust me. I'll be discreet."

"I've always trusted you," she answered just before his mouth covered hers, melting her resistance as well as her good intentions.

Carol rose onto her toes, and her arms tightened around his neck to bring his face closer. Her lips parted, inviting his invasion, but instead he jerked his head up, breaking the contact, and pushed her away.

"I'll see you tomorrow," he said brusquely and pulled open the door, shutting it behind him as he strode out.

Carol stood staring after him, too stunned even to close her mouth.

* * *

Carol spent the next day exploring places that had been important to her when she'd lived there: the school where she'd been head cheerleader, homecoming queen and winner of two college scholarships she'd never used; the Elks hall, where she'd been crowned Miss Raindance before becoming first runner-up in the Miss Nebraska contest in Lincoln; and the white church with the high bell tower where she'd gone to Sunday school every week and where she and Bryce had been married on that glorious Saturday morning in June.

She'd never been as excited as she'd been that day, she thought as she walked up the church's front steps. The sun had been shining, the perpetual Nebraska wind had miraculously stilled, and the white satin gown that had cost her parents a small fortune at Brandeis in Omaha had set off her long black hair and given her the look of a dewy-eyed angel. Rosemarie had been her maid of honor in royal blue, and the three bridesmaids had worn identically styled gowns in powder blue. Baskets of colorful flowers had banked the altar and blue satin bows had marked the pews.

Now, standing in the doorway to the empty chapel, the memory of that day was vivid with the overflowing crowd of assembled friends and relatives, the scent of flowers and the sacred music played on the ancient organ that her father had had tuned for the occasion.

But most of all she remembered Bryce, standing at the altar with his elder brother, watching her as she walked slowly down the aisle on her father's arm. She'd never seen him as handsome as he was in his formal wedding clothes, and his deep-set brown eyes brimmed with happiness and admiration and, most of all, love.

Carol blinked, and the long-ago scene was gone, replaced by the rather drab empty chapel. A fitting metaphor, she decided as she wiped away the two tears that had managed to squeeze out the corners of her eyes: by her own immature, thoughtless actions she'd blown away the magic in her life and replaced it with emotional austerity.

Carol had intended to wear jeans for her dinner with Bryce that evening. The sexual attraction between them was still strong, but he was fighting it and she knew he was appalled it was still there. He was going to marry Sharon, and if Carol tempted him beyond his considerable control, it wouldn't change anything. He'd still marry the other woman, and Carol would still be alone—but they'd share a heavy load of guilt. As she'd told him before, she already had all of that she could handle.

Still, after she'd showered and brushed her heavy shoulder-length hair until it shone like ebony, she couldn't bring herself to dress so casually. Instead she chose a loose-fitting turquoise gauze Mexican-style dress with a wide flounce on the skirt and a deep V neckline front and back, trimmed with cotton cro-cheted lace. Her legs were deeply tanned and it was too hot to wear panty hose, so she slipped her bare feet with their brightly manicured toenails into multicol-ored low-heeled sandals.

Bryce arrived on the stroke of seven, and his ad-miring gaze traveled over her, but he didn't comment as she shut and locked the door. He was wearing dove-gray tailored slacks and a red-and-gray print sport shirt open at the neck. Carol forced herself not to gape.

When she'd decided to come back to Raindance, she'd almost hoped to find Bryce with a paunch, thinning hair and ill-fitting clothes. Instead his belly was flat and hard, his slacks were hand-tailored and fit like a second skin, hinting at equally hard thighs, and his thick blond hair had darkened slightly but was styled with a side part and a shock that tumbled enticingly over his forehead. He was even sexier than she'd remembered, and that took some doing!

He headed the Thunderbird toward the business district but turned north on Cedar, the street where her family home was located.

"Where are we going?" she asked. To the best of her knowledge there were no restaurants in this area.

Bryce looked at her and grinned. "We're going to my parents' house."

Carol gasped in dismay. "Oh, Bryce, I don't think..."

Her in-laws had been just as upset and unforgiving toward her eight years ago as their son had been, and they'd made no effort to get in touch with her since she'd been back, although they must have known where she was staying. They'd been almost like second parents to her when she was growing up, and she'd have welcomed a chance to see and visit with them again. However, she hadn't been able to force herself to make the first move. They'd been so bitter that she'd felt it was best not to stir up the past. If they wanted to see her they'd have given some sign, but they hadn't.

"It's all right," Bryce said, as though he'd been reading her thoughts. "They're out of town. They left yesterday to spend a couple of weeks with Hilary and her family in Cheyenne.''

Hilary was Bryce's older sister. "Oh. How is Hilary?''

"She's fine. They're still ranching in the Cheyenne area, and both the kids are teenagers now.''

"Really? It doesn't seem possible. And Derek? How's he?'' Derek was Bryce and Hilary's brother—the one who had been best man at their wedding.

"He's fine, too. He and his family are still living in Chicago, and he's a grandfather now.''

"Oh, no!'' Carol groaned. "I guess none of us are getting any younger.''

"No, we're not, but the years have been kind to you. You were always a beauty, but something's been added. A softness, an empathy you didn't used to have. Why haven't you married again, Carol?''

The question took her off guard, and she answered before she thought. "I have a husband.''

The car swerved and she fell against him. "You what! You told me—''

She clutched at his arm to steady herself as he righted the auto. "No, you don't understand! I meant you. Oh, darn, why can't I keep my big mouth shut?''

By then they'd reached their destination, and Bryce swung into the driveway of his parents' home. He activated the automatic door opener and drove into the two-car garage.

He turned off the motor and put the keys in his pocket, then faced Carol. "I think you'd better explain.'' His voice was calm, but his hands still gripped the steering wheel.

She released his arm and backed away. "I'm sorry. I shouldn't have said that. I just wasn't thinking. I haven't married because I haven't had the time or the inclination. I was in school—and working—for almost six years, and for the last two I've spent most of my time struggling to advance in my profession."

He wasn't placated. "Then why did you say you have a husband?" His tone was heating up with anger.

She shook her head. "I shouldn't have said what I did, but I meant it. You're my husband, Bryce. You divorced me—I didn't divorce you. I know it's stupid of me, but I can't seem to think of myself as being free."

She had to get out of the car, away from the tension, and she pushed down on the door handle. "Look, just forget it, okay? I've never met another man I wanted to marry, so it's not important."

She stepped out into the garage.

As Bryce unlocked the door that led from the garage into the house, Carol was glad he'd chosen to go in this way rather than through the front where the neighbors would undoubtedly have seen him escorting his ex-wife into his parents' house and counted the time they stayed there.

As soon as she stepped into the familiar kitchen she smelled the mouth-watering aroma of Bryce's favorite meal, beef stew. She turned to him, surprised. "Who's doing the cooking?"

He was watching her with a wary, puzzled expression. "I am," he said absently. "I live alone, so I had to learn how to cook."

She couldn't seem to tear her gaze away from his. "As I remember, you learned to cook when you were married to me," she said sadly. "It was either that or subsist on peanut-butter sandwiches and ice cream."

Bryce finally looked away. "Don't, Carol. Stop whipping yourself. That's all in the past and can't be changed, so it does no good to dredge it up. If you'd like to go in the living room and watch television I'll finish getting dinner ready."

If he'd deliberately taunted her it couldn't have hurt more. He still didn't believe that she'd changed. He was treating her like the inept wife she'd been, who'd watched television and let her husband fix his own dinner.

"I live alone, too, remember?" She spoke quietly, careful not to let the pain come through. "I've had to look after myself for the past eight years, and in that time I've learned to cook quite well. Please let me help."

He was standing at the stove stirring the stew and had his back to her. "If you like," he said formally. "There's lettuce and fresh vegetables in the fridge. How are you at tossing a salad?"

She grinned and headed for the refrigerator. "Highly experienced. Which kind of dressing do you prefer?"

The kitchen seemed smaller than Carol remembered. She and Bryce couldn't seem to work in it together without touching in some way—an accidental collision, a meeting of their hands as they reached into a drawer at the same time or a brush of her shoulder against his arm as they stood side by side at the sink. Each time it happened her whole nervous system responded with a wave of heat, and by the time dinner was ready she was perspiring even though the air conditioner was on.

They ate at the antique round oak dining-room table, and their places were set side by side. Bryce was telling her about the cattlemen's meeting that he'd attended that day, but she was having a hard time concentrating because his left knee and her right arm kept rubbing together.

She wasn't doing it on purpose, and from the way he jerked his away when it happened she was sure he wasn't either. It was as if the two knees were magnetized and couldn't get close without clinging. Every time it happened he stumbled over his words, and she lost track of what he was saying.

"It's been quite an eye-opener," he concluded. "As we suspected, someone's buying up large amounts of Sandhills land and is doing it with as little public notice as possible. I'm sure now that we can get your mother considerably more money for her property if we hold out until we can discover what's going on."

Carol's nerves were raw and screaming for the relief that could only be gained by twining her aching body with the long hard length of his. She swallowed the last of her burgundy. "I can't tell you how grateful Mom and I are to you." Even her voice was shaking. "Mom really needs the money. Dad left her well-off, but she requires more and more care as her arthritis becomes more crippling, and eventually she'll have to go to a convalescent hospital."

Again their legs brushed together, but this time Bryce groaned and put his hand under the table to hold her knee against his. She caught her breath as his fingers caressed her inner thigh. "Don't fight it, sweetheart," he said huskily. "It's a losing battle."

He pushed his chair away from the table and held his hands out to her. She swiftly moved onto his lap, and he cuddled her close as his lips teased her throat. One hand cupped her breast and the other rested on her hip. His breathing was raspy, and the hardness that pressed against her bottom told her that his desire was as strong as hers. "I want the rest of that kiss we started last night," he murmured raggedly.

Carol's whole body tingled as she put her arms around his neck. "But you were the one who broke it off." Her face was only inches from his, and his breath was warm on her cheek.

"And you know why." He kissed her eyes shut. "If I hadn't I'd have spent the night making love to you."

She kept her lids closed as his lips roamed tenderly over her cheeks and forehead. "Is something different now?" She sounded as breathless as she felt.

"Mmm-mm." He sounded breathless, too. "My self-control is back in working order. Last night I was frantic and couldn't think straight."

She caressed his jaw line with her tongue, tasting his salty skin. "I'm glad yours is so strong, because mine is slipping badly."

His moan was muffled against her mouth as he covered it with his own.

Chapter Eight

They broke the kiss only when the need to breathe demanded it, and even then Bryce felt like a man too long denied water, who couldn't get enough once it was offered.

He took a deep breath and claimed Carol's lips again, desperate for the sustenance that only she could give, that made his blood race, his heart pound and his loins throb. No other woman had ever been able to arouse him the way she did, and it had been so long, so agonizingly long.

For eight interminable years he'd yearned for this woman—and despised himself for his weakness. No man worthy of the name would let a woman treat him the way she had and then come back for more. It was madness. But, dear God, how was he going to find the strength to send her away again?

When he finally managed to lift his head and breathe a second time, he looked down at her. Her face was turned up to his, and her eyes were still closed. Her cheeks were flushed with emotion, and although she was greedily gasping in air, an involuntary murmur of protest escaped her.

It was her total responsiveness that shook him to the depth of his soul. During their courtship she'd held back, let him go only so far, and at times when the frustration was almost unbearable he'd accused her of teasing. It was only after their wedding, when they'd finally been alone together, that he'd learned the depth of her passion.

He shivered with the memory, and she opened her eyes and blinked. He knew he had to break the magnetism between them or he was not only going to make love to her, but he was going to do it right there on the dining-room carpet.

It took a lot of willpower, but he managed to loosen his hold on her. "Maybe we'd better have our coffee now," he said, and his voice sounded like it had traveled over ground glass. "I'll bring it into the living room."

She slid off his lap, and he noticed that her face was flaming. "Yes." Her tone was ragged, too, and she turned and walked into the other room.

Bryce brought their mugs and sat down on the sofa beside Carol. He wrapped both hands around his heavy ironstone cup and brought it to his mouth. He could have used a shot of something stronger in it, but, although liquor may have calmed him down a little, it would also have lowered his resistance, and he needed all of that he could muster.

Carol took a large swallow of her coffee and hoped it would empty enough of the mug so her trembling hands wouldn't spill the rest.

She leaned her head against the back of the sofa and closed her eyes. How could Bryce sit beside her so calm and collected? Those kisses they'd shared had left her totally unglued. He was right. His self-control was working again with a vengeance. She wished hers was as reliable, but it wavered every time he looked at her, touched her—and when he kissed her it vanished altogether.

She felt his finger tracing a line down her cheek, and opened her eyes. He was hovering above her looking concerned. "Are you tired?" Again he kissed her eyes closed. "Did you have a busy day?"

She reached up and cupped his head with both hands and wove her fingers through his hair. "No, I'm not tired. Not physically. Maybe a little emotionally. It's been . . . traumatic coming back here."

She smiled as she continued to stroke him. "Today I took a tour of some of my old hangouts. The school, the church . . ."

Her voice broke, and Bryce gathered her in his arms and settled her head on his shoulder. "I haven't been in that church except for an occasional wedding or funeral since you left. Every time I go in there I see you coming down the aisle looking both virginal and seductive in that white gown."

He lowered his head and nuzzled the pulse that pounded at the side of her neck. "God, how I loved you." His voice was a tortured rasp.

Carol rubbed her palm over the left side of his chest and caressed his hard male nipple. *Loved.* Past tense. She'd killed all traces of the love that should have been so precious to her, leaving only lust in its place.

How could she have been so stupid?

"I loved you, too," she said, and tipped her head to make it easier for him to find other erogenous zones to explore. "I always loved you. I behaved abominably, and I understand that you couldn't live with me after what happened. But darling, I swear with God as my witness that I was never unfaithful to you."

He raised his head, and his hold on her loosened. "Dammit, Carol, don't lie to me. I told you before, it doesn't matter anymore. I managed to survive the agony of the whole state knowing I couldn't satisfy my wife in bed, and now I just don't give a damn."

He tried to push her away, but she clasped her arms firmly around his neck. "No, Bryce, please listen to me. I know this is painful to dredge up again, but you're never going to heal until you accept the truth."

He could have put her away from him if he'd been determined to, but he didn't try again. His arms were still around her, and his hands rested, without pressure, at her waist.

She stretched up and planted a small kiss on either side of his grimly set mouth, then began gently massaging the nape of his neck as she told him in the same way she'd told Sharon about the events of that night. She began with her anger when he'd had to work instead of taking her to the square dance and ended with her arrest. She didn't hold back anything or try to soften her part in the fiasco.

By the time she finished she was holding him in a loving embrace with his head nestled between her breasts, and her tone was an impassioned plea. "I had no idea Joel was sleeping beside me on that bed. The shock of everything that had happened plus the whiskey I'd drunk pretty much knocked me out, and I'd been more or less unconscious most of the night."

She kissed the top of his head and caressed his cheek with her hand. "That doesn't excuse me for the way I behaved or make it any more worthy of forgiveness, but I don't ever want you to think that you couldn't satisfy me with our lovemaking. It was beautiful— everything I'd ever dreamed about—until I spoiled it."

He didn't comment, just slid the bodice of her loose-fitting dress down until the low neckline exposed one lace-covered breast. She gasped with pleasure as his hand cupped it. "You've matured physically," he murmured, completely changing the subject as his lips caressed the creamy swelling. "Your waist and hips are slimmer, but your breasts are fuller, riper. How I've yearned to fit them in my palms again, to feel them against my chest, soft and warm, to taste their sweetness and feel the nipples harden."

He unhooked the front fastener on her bra and pushed it aside so he could fondle the already hard peak with his tongue. Muscles deep within her contracted, and she whimpered softly as her fingers dug into his shoulders. "Ha-have you really yearned for me?" she asked, wanting to believe but afraid he was simply carried away by the moment.

He tensed and raised his head to look at her. "You like that idea, don't you?" His tone was hard. "You always reveled in the power you had over me—and misused it."

She could have cried with frustration. "Oh, Bryce, don't misread everything I say. I just meant I didn't think you'd even thought of me, let alone yearned for me. You were so full of rage and hate when I left here."

He glared at her. "And with good reason, wouldn't you say?" He sat up and pushed her away. "You're right, it was just passion talking. Haven't you learned about men by now? They'll say anything to make a woman more responsive at a time like that."

Carol cringed as the jab hit deep and true, but she wasn't going to let him get away with it. "Wasn't I responsive enough for you?" she asked, as she refastened her bra and straightened the top of her dress. "Sorry, I didn't realize you wanted a quickie. I'm a little out of practice, but I'm sure you can find someone to accommodate you."

She jumped up and headed for the kitchen, with Bryce right behind her. "Carol!" He grabbed her by the arm and swung her around. His eyes were filled with regret. "I'm sorry. That was rotten of me. You've got me in such a state that I don't know what I'm doing or saying. Part of the time I want to punish you, and the rest of the time I'd sell my soul just to be near you, to touch you, to have you touch me."

He put his arms around her and drew her close, and she didn't seem able to resist. He was so obviously tormented by conflicting desires. "I need you, sweetheart." The confession seemed torn out of him. "I'm burning up with need for you, but I'm terrified of giving in to it. If I do and find you haven't changed after all, it will destroy me. I couldn't survive a second betrayal."

Carol understood, and she knew it was perfectly rational for him to distrust her. She would have felt the same if their positions had been reversed, but it tore her apart to see him so anguished.

She put her arms around his waist and rested her cheek against his chest. "I love you, Bryce. That's never changed, but I can understand why you don't

believe me. I guess all I can do for you now is try not
to mess up your life any more than I already have.''

She rubbed her palms over the hard flesh and muscles of his back. "I'll load the dishwasher, and then
you can take me home. It's best if we don't see each
other again while I'm here unless it's absolutely necessary.''

His arms tightened around her. "You don't have to
do the dishes.''

She continued to rub his back. "Sure I do. You
cooked the dinner, it's only fair that I clean up afterward.''

"If we stay here any longer,'' he said, his voice
tightly controlled, "I'm going to make love to you—
now.''

Oh, if only he would instead of just talking about it,
Carol cried inwardly. But if he did he'd be sure she'd
seduced him, and that's something she'd promised
Sharon she wouldn't do. She'd go to Bryce if he seri-
ously wanted her, but she wouldn't break the promise
she'd made to his fianceé. It was a pretty shaky sense
of honor, but it was the best she could do. Bryce was
her man, and she felt no guilt at wanting him back.

She forced a chuckle. "Promises, promises,'' she
said lightly, and moved out of his arms and through
the door to the car.

Carol was sound asleep and had been for hours
when the shrill ring of the telephone roused her. For a
moment she lay there listening to it until she finally
wakened enough to realize it was her phone and she'd
better answer it.

She reached toward the bedside table in the dark
and fumbled for several seconds before her hand fi-

nally found the receiver. She picked it up and snuggled it against her ear. "Hello." It sounded more like a yawn than a greeting.

"Is this Carol Garrett?" It was a male voice, but not one she immediately recognized.

"Yes, who's this? What time is it?"

This time she fumbled for the lamp as the voice on the other end answered. "Carol, this is Jim Perkins. You know, Rosemarie's husband."

She finally found the switch and turned on the light. The travel alarm read 4:26. "Yes, of course Jim." She was awake enough now to be apprehensive. "What's the matter?"

"I'm sorry to wake you in the middle of the night," he said, and for the first time she recognized the anxiety in his voice. "Is Rosemarie with you by any chance?"

"No." She sat up and swung her feet over the side of the bed. "For heaven's sake, Jim, it's four-thirty in the morning. Do you mean she's not home?"

"I—Have you seen her at all since dinnertime?"

A feeling of dread knotted her stomach muscles. "No. I went out for dinner and didn't get back here until around ten, but I haven't seen or heard from her since then. Jim, what's wrong? Why isn't she there with you?"

"Oh, Lord, I don't know." Jim was thoroughly upset. "We had a quarrel and she stormed out of here shortly after dinner. She took the car and she hasn't come back. We only have the one car, and besides I can't leave the kids alone. I'm worried sick. I hate to start calling people in the middle of the night like this, but—"

Carol was now on her feet. "Jim, listen to me. Don't call anyone else just yet. I'll put on some clothes and be right over. You can take my car to look for her, and I'll stay with the children. See you inside of ten minutes."

She put the phone in its cradle and grabbed a pair of jeans and a knit shirt out of the dresser drawer.

Jim's dark eyes looked a little wild when he opened the door to her knock, and his sandy hair stood on end as though he'd been running his fingers through it. "Thanks for coming," he said quickly. "Rosie has never done a thing like this before. I'm terrified that she may have had an accident or something."

He took the keys she handed him and started out the door. "Oh, I was just dialing Bryce's number when you arrived. Would you please do it for me? Explain what's happened, and ask him if he'll cover the west half of town and watch for the car. If she's staying with someone it will be parked nearby. I'll take the east side."

He ran out without giving her a chance to answer.

So much for not getting in touch with Bryce again, she thought as she dialed the number that had been her own for two years.

The phone at the other end rang for quite awhile before it was finally answered by an obviously sleepy Bryce. "Garrett residence."

"Bryce, this is Carol."

"Carol?" The sleepiness was gone from his voice. "What's wrong? Are you all right?"

"I'm fine. It's not me, it's Rosemarie." She told him what had happened and relayed Jim's request. "Jim's nearly out of his mind, and I'm worried, too. She's pregnant again and not happy about it. I had a long talk with her the other day, and she's pretty up-set about a lot of things."

Bryce swore. "I'll leave right away and check in with you from time to time. Did she give any indication she intended to do something like this?"

"No, none. It must have been a spur-of-the-moment decision."

They hung up, and Carol rummaged around in the kitchen until she found the essential equipment to make coffee. While it was dripping she went into the bathroom and brushed her teeth with the toothbrush she'd brought with her and combed her hair. Tepid water splashed on her face brought some color to her cheeks and made her eyes brighter. She wanted to look reasonably presentable in case the little boys woke up and she had to deal with them.

By seven o'clock the two men had combed the town and the surrounding area with no luck. There was no sign of the two-tone brown 1985 Chevrolet Celebrity on any of the streets, alleys or rural side roads.

The three of them were sitting in the kitchen having coffee and looking grim. Jim rubbed his ravaged face with his hands and sighed. "I don't know why Rosie would do a thing like this," he said raggedly. "She hasn't been feeling well lately, but it's just morning sickness."

Carol tensed. *Just* morning sickness! Only a man would make that statement. How did he manage to live with Rosemarie through two pregnancies without discovering that morning sickness can be a continuous nausea day and night for several months?

Bryce spoke. "Maybe it would help if you told us what you two quarreled about. I don't mean to pry, but—"

"That's okay," Jim assured him. "To tell you the truth I'm not sure what brought it on. I have two weeks' vacation coming up soon, and today I got a chance to rent a cabin at Merritt Lake. The rent was reasonable and the fishing up there is great, so I took it. I guess I should have called Rosie first, but..."

Carol was appalled. She knew the Merritt Lake area, approximately seventy miles west of Raindance. It was open rolling Sandhills country with no shade or convenience of any kind. Thirty miles from the nearest town, it was excellent fishing for sportsmen, but would be a disaster as a vacation spot for a woman with two small children to look after.

"Oh, Jim," she groaned. "I'll bet I can tell you exactly what happened next. You told her and she was furious. She probably said that all she'd get out of it was sweltering heat, mosquitoes and double the amount of work. That she'd be totally isolated, with two little kids to try to prevent from drowning in the lake while you spent the days fishing. That she'd have to cook on a camp stove, pump and heat water every time she needed it and clean your damn fish."

Jim's mouth dropped open. "How did you know?"

Carol couldn't believe he could be so dense. "Because it's exactly what I would have said, and I'd have left you, too. How could you be so totally uncaring about what *she* wanted?"

Bryce held up his hands and tried to say something but was drowned out by Jim, who jumped out of his chair and glared at Carol. "Who in hell are you to call me selfish?" he demanded. "You cornered the market on that behavior a long time ago, you little—"

A loud bang cut off his words as Bryce stood, hitting the table with the palm of his hand. "Don't say it, Jim," he warned, and his voice was lethal.

He turned to look at Carol. "Right now Jim needs understanding, not condemnation. If you can't give him that then I suggest you go back to the motel."

Jim dropped back down in his chair, and Carol looked away. "I'm sorry, Jim," she said. "Bryce is right, I came on too strong, but I'm frightened, too. Rosie's at a point in her life when she's feeling trapped by diapers and bottles and never enough time. She's probably at a low ebb physically, as well. Pregnancy makes a lot of demands on a woman's body, and when it comes along every couple of years or oftener it can take a toll. It's not your fault, but it's not hers, either. She needs a lot of tender loving care right now."

Jim dropped his face in his hands. "It never occurred to me that she wasn't as happy with our family as I am." His tone was rough with regret.

Carol stood and went around the table to put her arm around his shoulders. "She loves you and the children—don't ever doubt that—but she needs to be a person in her own right, not just your wife and the children's mother. All I'm saying is that she needs to be treated like an adult, an equal partner in your marriage, and not like an older child. I'm sure she'll tell you the same thing when she's cooled down and comes home."

Just then the sound of the front door being opened and closed brought Jim to his feet so quickly that he almost knocked Carol over. He tore out of the kitchen, but Bryce and Carol weren't far behind. From the dining room they had a clear view of the living room and Jim and Rosemarie fused together in an embrace that made it plain they no longer needed either help or company.

Bryce put his hand at the small of Carol's back, and they returned to the kitchen and closed the door. "I'm afraid we've just become superfluous," he said with a smile.

"I think you're right," Carol agreed, grinning back at him.

He glanced at his watch and swore. "I've got an appointment at the office in fifteen minutes, and I have to go home and shower and change first." He looked at Carol and his face softened. "Thanks for coming so fast when Jim needed you. He'll thank you himself when he's a little more coherent."

Carol basked in Bryce's approval. "Rosie used to be my best friend. I wanted to help. Besides, you were the one who did all the searching. I just loaned Jim my car and stayed here so the children wouldn't be alone."

The appreciation on his face disappeared, and his expression hardened. "I owe Jim more than I can ever repay," he said tightly. "He was there when I needed him eight years ago. Believe me, I know how he felt when his wife didn't come home."

Carol cringed at his swift change of mood. She should be used to it by now, but the pain it caused never lessened. He'd erected the wall between them again and had withdrawn behind it.

"Goodbye," he said without expression, and left by the back door.

Carol left a few minutes later.

It wasn't until the next morning that Carol heard from either Jim or Rosemarie, and then it was Rosemarie who phoned. "I don't know how I can ever thank you for pitching in and helping during our family crisis night before last. I—I'm so embarrassed."

"Don't be," Carol answered. "I'm just glad I was here and able to help. How are you? Is everything all right now?"

"I'm fine." Rosemarie's voice had a happy bounce to it. "Jim and I finally sat down and really talked, but we'll tell you all about it tonight. We want you to have dinner with us. I know it's short notice, but Bryce and Sharon will be able to make it and we're counting on you to be here, too."

Bryce and Sharon. Oh dear, that was bound to be uncomfortable at best. She hadn't seen Bryce's fiancée since Monday when they'd had lunch together and Carol had bared her soul, so to speak, Sharon had been distinctly cool by the time Carol had left, and by now she'd know that Bryce had been with Carol in the middle of the night trying to find Rosemarie while Sharon had been excluded. It hadn't occurred to Carol to call her at the time, and she was sure Bryce hadn't thought of it either.

"Carol, are you still there?" Rosemarie sounded uncertain. "Please say you'll come. Jim and I are so grateful to you and Bryce that we want to thank you properly and tell you how we've resolved the problem. You will come, won't you?"

There was no way she could gracefully get out of it. "Yes, of course I will, Rosie. Thank you for asking me. But are you sure you feel up to it?"

Rosemarie laughed. "You bet. I'm fixing pot roast with potatoes and carrots. The whole thing can be cooked in one pot, and Jim has ordered a pie from the bakery. Is seven-thirty okay? That'll give me a chance to feed the kids and put them down first.''

Carol was dressed in the blue silky gown she'd worn to the dance on Sunday and had just picked up her purse to leave when the phone rang. It was her mother wanting to chat, so she arrived about fifteen minutes late at the Perkinses' home for dinner. Bryce's Thunderbird was parked in the driveway, so she knew he and Sharon must already be there.

Rosemarie answered the door and hugged her as she stepped inside. "I'm so sorry to be late," Carol apologized, "but Mom called from California just as I was leaving."

"That's okay, we just got the kids to bed anyway," Rosemarie said as she and Carol entered the living room.

Bryce and Jim stood as the women appeared, and Jim came over and hugged Carol, too, then put his arm across her shoulders. "Come to the kitchen with me and tell me what you want to drink." He led her off before she had a chance to say hello to the other couple.

In the kitchen with the door closed he dropped his arm and walked over to the counter where there were several bottles of liquor and mixes. "What'll you have? If it's anything too complicated you'll have to tell me how to make it." He seemed uncomfortable in her company.

"Vodka and orange juice, please," she said, and wondered why he'd brought her out here when he could just as well have taken her order in the living room.

He went to the refrigerator and got a pitcher of orange juice. "I owe you an apology, Carol, and my deepest gratitude." He still didn't look at her, and it dismayed her to think he disliked her so much that being in her debt upset him.

"You don't owe me anything, Jim," she said coolly. "Rosemarie's a special friend, and I'm just glad I was able to help. I'm not a gossip, if that's what's bothering you. I won't mention the episode to anyone."

He set the vodka bottle down with a bang and turned to face her. "Oh, hey, that's not what I meant. Damn, I'm really botching this, aren't I."

She looked back at him, troubled. "Yes, I guess you are. Did Rosie tell you you had to apologize to me? I'd rather you didn't. Some of the things I said to you were really out of line, and I don't blame you for being mad."

His face registered shock. "Is that what you think? Hell, I'm so damn grateful to you I'd crawl on my knees to ask your forgiveness for the way I've been behaving if that's what you wanted. I was at my wits' end when I called you, and you didn't even make me ask. You volunteered to let me use your car and to stay with the kids. Then, when you tried to tell me what I'd done wrong and I blew up at you, you tried to comfort me."

He ran his hands through his hair. "If Rosie hadn't come home just then I'd have cried in your arms like a baby. Carol, I'm trying to apologize for being such a jackass and thank you for helping me to straighten out the mess I'd made of things...."

She felt weak with relief. The fact that the people in her hometown disapproved of her bothered her more than she liked to admit, even to herself.

Jim had finally forgiven her. Or had he? He said he wanted to apologize, not forgive. Maybe she'd better bring it out in the open so there wouldn't be any more misunderstandings.

"I was happy to help, Jim, but I'm sure you still have a lot of reservations about me, and there's something I want you to know."

She looked straight into his eyes. "I was never unfaithful to Bryce with Joel or anyone else. I was guilty of bad judgment, indiscretion and colossal stupidity, but never of adultery. I had no need to play around. I had all the loving I could ever want at home, and it was fantastic until I ruined everything."

She found it difficult to say these things to Jim. Carol wasn't in the habit of discussing her sex life with anyone. It was private, personal and, in the last few years, nonexistent. She knew she was blushing, and Jim shifted uneasily, too.

"Well, at least you're outspokenly honest," he said. "I'm sure that makes Bryce feel better."

"Bryce doesn't believe me. I've told him exactly what happened, but he didn't even comment."

Jim picked up her drink and handed it to her. "Maybe it's just as well." He was choosing his words carefully, but he couldn't screen out the disapproval in his tone. "It took Bryce years to get over what you did to him. For a long time he wouldn't even date, and when he finally did start he wouldn't go out with the same woman twice in a row."

He picked up a bottle of bourbon and poured some of it into an empty glass. "It wasn't until he started seeing Sharon that he seemed to relax and trust again. The day they became engaged was a day of rejoicing for his friends—and that includes the whole town.

Sharon is exactly what he needs. He's suffered enough, and she's quiet, reserved and dependable."

He took a long swallow of the whiskey. "If you still have any feelings for Bryce you'll leave town, Carol," he said gently. "Go back to California and leave him in peace. I've noticed the torment he tries to hide whenever he sees you or your name is mentioned. You're starting it up all over again, but he'd never be happy with you. He can't trust you, and he'd go crazy trying to live with you without trust."

Jim's tone of voice was calm, reasonable, even kind, but Carol felt as if she'd been flayed. Nobody was willing to believe she'd learned her lesson and wouldn't make the same mistake again. It was no use protesting that she loved Bryce and would die before she hurt him again. She'd never live down her past.

She was still reeling when Jim delivered his final blow. "Do the poor guy a favor, Carol, and go home to Los Angeles. Give Sharon a chance. She'll make him happy. You never will."

Chapter Nine

Before Carol could answer Jim the door opened and Bryce strode in. "What's going on out here?" His tone was tinged with irritation. "It doesn't take fifteen minutes to pour a drink."

They must have both looked guilty, because Bryce paused and his eyes narrowed. "Am I interrupting something?"

Jim found his voice first. "Yes, as a matter of fact you are," he said testily. "I was just thanking Carol for her help. What have you been doing, holding a stopwatch on us?" He didn't smile when he said it.

Bryce was looking at Carol. "Are you all right? What's he been saying to you?" He sounded angry.

She knew she must look as stricken as she felt. She swallowed and made a determined effort to sound cheerful. "I'm fine, but you're right, we should join the others. I imagine Rosemarie's waiting to serve dinner." She walked out of the kitchen ahead of them.

The roast beef Carol had been smelling ever since she'd stepped into the house was tender and delicately spiced, and the rest of the meal was just as delicious. The conversation revolved around current events, both nationwide and in Raindance, and Carol's position with the television station's public relations department, which seemed to be of great interest to the others.

The climate between Sharon and Carol was cool but friendly. As usual, Sharon was the perfect lady. Only she and Carol could tell that their relationship was strained. Carol was reserved in her rapport with Bryce, friendly but distant, although she knew he was still puzzled about the scene in the kitchen.

They had cherry pie and coffee in the living room, and it was then that Jim and Rosemarie got to the reason for the gathering. They were sitting close together on the sofa when Rosemarie set her half-eaten pie on the coffee table and said, "Jim and I asked you here so we could thank you for giving up most of a night's sleep because of my silly temper tantrum—"

Jim interrupted. "It wasn't silly, and it was all my fault. I don't know how I could have been so blind to Rosie's needs, and if Carol hadn't pointed it out to me I'd still be groping around wondering what happened."

"But that's just the point, darling." Rosemarie put her arm through her husband's and snuggled against his side. "I should have discussed things with you long ago instead of bottling it all up inside until it exploded."

Jim kissed the top of her head. "We were both to blame, but we've had a long talk and straightened out a lot of things."

He looked at Carol and grinned. "You'll be happy to know that our vacation plans have been changed. Rosie's mother and sister are going to look after the boys while we spend ten days in Hawaii. We'll be all by ourselves in a first-class hotel, and Rosie won't have to lift a finger to do anything."

Jim and Rosemarie beamed, and so did everyone else. "Oh, that sounds marvelous!" Carol cried joyfully. "I'll have to admit, Jim, when you put your mind to it you really know how to plan a great vacation."

"Second honeymoon," Jim corrected her as he put his arm around his wife. "Even though we will be accompanied by our third child."

He patted Rosemarie's stomach, and his smile grew even wider as he shrugged. "What can I say? I can't keep my hands off the lady."

"It took more than hands, love," Rosemarie said slyly, and everyone burst into laughter.

When they'd settled down a little Rosemarie said, "I just hope that by the time we leave for Hawaii I'll be over the morning sickness but not yet into maternity clothes."

She looked at Sharon and grinned. "See what you've got ahead of you when you and Bryce start your family?"

The thin, bone-china cup and saucer in Carol's hand shook, making a clattering noise. She set it down hastily, hoping nobody had noticed the way her muscles had jerked. The very mention of Sharon having Bryce's babies was agony. That should have been her privilege—would have been if she hadn't thrown it away.

Her hands were shaking and she wanted to leave, but her legs were trembling, too. She wasn't going to make a spectacle of herself by falling at Bryce's feet.

She glanced over at him, and their eyes met. She looked away quickly. Had he noticed her reaction to Rosie's statement? Was her anguish right there on her face for all to see?

She took a deep breath and pushed herself up out of her chair. Thank goodness her unsteady legs seemed willing to support her.

She pasted a smile on her face. "Thanks for inviting me over Rosie, Jim. The dinner was delicious, and I've enjoyed the visit so much."

"You're not leaving?" Rosemarie's tone was filled with dismay as the two men rose. "But it's early yet. We'd planned a game of bridge, or canasta."

"You've got enough people for cards without me," she said reassuringly, "and I have to get back to the room and wash out some clothes. I didn't bring many changes with me."

Rosemarie got up and came over to embrace Carol. "I wish you'd stay." Her tone was wistful.

"I'll see you again before I leave. I'm glad everything has worked out so well for you and Jim."

Jim was standing beside them. "We realize that overcoming our problems isn't as simple as a second honeymoon," he said. "We've arranged to see a marriage counselor in Omaha next week, and we'll keep working on it."

He, too, embraced her. "Hang in there, honey," he said softly, "and I hope all your dreams come true."

"No, you don't," she murmured into his ear, knowing he'd understand that what she wanted was Bryce. She pulled back gently and looked across the room at Bryce and Sharon. "Goodbye, you two," she called, then turned and fled.

The summer heat continued unabated the next day, but Carol couldn't stand the depressing little room for long. She put on her red shorts, applied insect repellent liberally to her bare arms and legs and went for another walk.

She was in the vicinity of the church when the Sunday services let out, and she stood in the shade of a huge old oak across the highway where she could watch without being noticed. She saw friends and acquaintances stroll out of the white frame building after shaking hands at the door with the minister, who was new since she'd lived here. The congregants were dressed in lightweight summer clothes, and most of the men hadn't bothered with jackets or ties.

Tom and Donna Trent, looking cheerful, came down the steps and stopped to talk to Miss Dillingham, the timid little spinster who'd been the town librarian for forty years. A few minutes later Carol spied Jim and Rosemarie coming out of the Sunday school wing with their two young sons. It occurred to Carol that she'd never seen the Perkinses' children before. They'd always been gone or asleep when she'd been at their house.

They were adorable towheaded tots dressed alike in short pants and pullover shirts. She felt a stab of envy as the little group walked along, Jim carrying the younger son and Rosemarie holding the hand of the elder. They looked like the subjects of a Norman Rockwell painting—the perfect young family. Even though Carol knew that wasn't altogether true, at least the potential was there. Carol's own chances of a happy marriage and children were fading with time.

She almost missed seeing Sharon Davis, who was one of the last to emerge. She was wearing a navy linen two-piece dress and navy-and-white spectator pumps. Her glasses' lenses had darkened and shaded her eyes from the glare of the sun. Sharon was one of those fortunate people who looked pretty both with and without her glasses. She stopped to talk to the Perkinses, and after a few minutes they separated and went in opposite directions to their cars.

Carol turned and walked away. She'd like to have been a part of that group. In a village the size of Raindance the churches were an integral part of the community's social life. Their members held rummage sales, monthly luncheons, parties for children and teenagers—not to mention potluck dinners, the older women's quilting circle and the young married couples' club. Once she'd been in the very center of these activities, but now she was standing on the other side of the road looking in.

She recrossed the highway at the next crosswalk and had walked a block before she realized where she was headed. If she went another block north and a half a block east she'd come to the house she and Bryce had lived in while they were married. Their home.

Her footsteps lagged, but she didn't stop. She'd been avoiding this place ever since she'd been back, wanting to see it but unwilling to endure the pain that calling up those old ghosts would inflict.

Her brain screamed at her to stop, go back, let the past stay buried, but her heart urged her forward, pumping its determination into her legs, which kept moving, left, right, left, right....

When she came to the crossroads where she had to decide whether to go ahead, turn east or go back, she stopped. Again, the sensible part of her brain tugged at her to go straight, but her romantic heart seemed to pound the message, *turn east, turn east. Don't run away.*

She looked down the street. In the middle of the block the screened-in front porch and the lawn, green and neatly trimmed, were visible. Bryce had always liked working in the yard, and obviously he still kept it well tended.

There was no car on the street in front of the house or in the driveway, and without fully realizing she'd made a decision, Carol started walking down the block. The big elm tree still shaded the front of the house, and Bryce had planted rose bushes, which bloomed in colorful profusion along the porch.

Carol paused on the sidewalk, then took a few steps onto the lawn and leaned back against the thick, rough trunk of the tree. She was facing the house, hidden from the street. The air around her was sweltering, and the old elm's shade was a blessed relief. A small breeze rustled the limbs and they brushed against her in what she'd like to think was a hug of welcome.

She reached out and patted the nearest one, and it bit her—at least that's what it felt like when a split in the wood pinched her finger. Well, why not? Apparently the tree wasn't about to forgive her either.

She heard a car coming down the street and decided she'd better move on before someone saw her loitering there like a lovesick adolescent mooning over the place where her current heartthrob lived. But she was too late. The car that turned into the driveway was Bryce's!

She felt trapped and distinctly unwelcome when she saw the scowl on his face as he got out of the car. "What are you doing here?" His tone was gruff.

"I—I went for a walk and... well... I hadn't seen the house since I came back, so..." Her voice trailed off, and there was silence between them.

Silence, and something else. Tension. Bryce had come across the yard to stand in front of her, and the stinging awareness that was always there when they were together seemed doubly charged this morning.

He was dressed in faded jeans, and the errant lock of blond hair tumbled over his forehead, making her fingers ache to brush it back and feel its lively springiness. His brown eyes were expressionless as they roamed over her from the top of her cascading black hair to her jutting breasts beneath the snug red-and-white knit top, her narrow waist and flaring hips encased in short shorts, her long bare legs and white Reeboks.

"I don't want you in my house, Carol," he said gruffly. "It took me years to exorcise you. To stop expecting to see you when I stepped through a doorway or hear your voice in the next room."

She felt his pain as well as her own, and it was almost more than she could bear. "I understand," she said softly, but she knew her eyes were shimmering with unshed tears. "I hadn't expected to go in. I didn't think anyone was home. I'd better go."

She turned and started to walk away, but Bryce's hand clamped around her wrist. "Come on," he barked, and practically dragged her to the front door.

Carol was too astonished to protest as he unlocked it and led her into the living room. He let go of her, and they stood side by side in the pleasantly cool house as she slowly surveyed the room. It wasn't large. The whole house was small, yet big enough for two. From where she stood she could also see the dining room, and the furniture in both areas was the same as when she'd left except more worn. Bryce had painted the walls white and removed most of the pictures and knickknacks she'd had sitting around, which had created a more masculine look.

"If I'd known I was going to have company I'd have straightened up around here," he said, and gathered up the sections of the Sunday *Omaha World Herald* that were scattered on the sofa and coffee table.

She dampened her dry lips with the tip of her tongue and hoped her voice wouldn't break. "It looks fine."

"You're probably thirsty after walking so far in this heat. Do you want something to drink? Iced tea? Soda? Coffee?" Avoiding looking at her, he continued to move around the room, straightening things that didn't need to be straightened.

"Iced tea, if you have it ready." She still hadn't moved.

"Okay. You can take the tour of the house while I get it." He moved rapidly across the dining room and into the kitchen.

Carol followed him, more slowly, and found that, except for a new refrigerator to replace the second-hand one they'd had, everything was the same here, too. Even the blue-and-white wallpaper had survived, although it needed to be replaced. She remembered the mess they'd made when they'd put it up. They'd quarreled halfway through, then made up in bed and forgotten about the walls until the next day.

She swallowed the lump in her throat and retreated while Bryce wrestled with ice trays.

The hall had also been painted white, and the Elvis poster she'd tacked to the wall was gone. What a child she'd been. Now her condo walls were hung with original oils and watercolors by little-known but talented artists from the Los Angeles area, and Bryce had a couple of well-executed Western scenes hung in his living room.

The bedroom to the right, which had been a spare room, was now furnished as Bryce's home office. He'd built in bookcases clear across one wall, and she noted they were nearly filled with law books, textbooks on accounting, biographies, histories and a few adventure and suspense novels. On another wall was a large studio photograph of Sharon, looking quite lovely.

Carol backed out and hurried on to the bathroom at the end of the hall. It had been the room most in need of renovating when she'd lived there. Obviously Bryce had seen to it. The new tile was brown with beige trim, and the modern fixtures were a matching beige. The sink was set in the middle of a vanity with a large mirror on the wall behind. With all the improvements it didn't even look like the same room.

She hesitated before moving on to the master bedroom on the left of the hallway. She'd averted her eyes when she'd passed it, and she was tempted to do it again on her way back to the front rooms. That was the one place in the house where she and Bryce had been happiest, where they'd made up their differences and pledged their love anew. There had been few nights during their short marriage when they hadn't made love before they went to sleep, not to mention all the mornings, late afternoons. . . .

Carol mentally chastised herself and marched quickly past the open door, then stopped. She was running away again. If she didn't go in there it would always haunt her.

She turned around and took the few steps that put her in the doorway. Since she was looking down the first thing she saw was the highly polished hardwood floor, covered in the middle by the hand-braided rug made by Bryce's great-grandmother and given to them as a wedding gift by his grandmother. Carol hadn't fully appreciated it at the time, but now she realized what a precious heirloom it was.

Slowly she lifted her gaze, expecting to see the white-and-gold French-provincial-style bedroom suite she'd bought without Bryce's knowledge or agreement during one of her shopping sprees, but it was gone. In its stead was a double bed and chest of drawers in heavy solid oak. The ruffled pink bedspread and matching curtains had been replaced by fitted blinds at the windows and a plain woven spread with alternating stripes of brown, rust and gold.

It was spartan, monk-like and strictly masculine.

Carol slumped against the doorjamb, stunned. She'd dreaded revisiting the bedroom and seeing it as it had been when she'd occupied it with Bryce; of touching the dresser where he'd kept his underwear and socks; of looking again in the mirror above the dressing table where she'd watched Bryce undress behind her as she sat in one of her seductive nightgowns brushing her hair; of approaching the bed where they'd made such sweet and passionate love.

But this was a thousand times worse. Bryce had discarded her totally. She'd been banished without a trace, as if she'd never shared the room with him!

For a long time she stood staring, unable to look away or even to close her eyes. She wasn't aware that she was crying until the tears started tickling her neck, then she covered her face with her hands and sobbed silently.

Bryce filled the ice trays too full of water, then spilled part of it on the way back to the refrigerator. For the hundredth time he berated himself for not buying the one with an automatic ice maker. But then, when had he last made a rational intelligent decision? If he'd been using his head he'd have let Carol leave after he'd made it plain he didn't want her here.

He'd been as surprised as she when his hand reached out almost of its own accord and hauled her inside with him. Now, unless he acted fast to get her out, he was once again going to be haunted by her presence in these rooms.

He took the pitcher of tea back to the counter and poured it in the glasses, then grabbed some paper towels to wipe up the floor. He'd been on fire for Carol ever since he'd succumbed to the temptation to do a little adult necking at his parents' house. He should have known that if he started something like that with Carol and didn't carry through he'd spend the rest of his life doing push-ups and taking cold showers!

Dammit, why was he putting himself through this? He knew she'd make love with him—she'd told him she would—and she'd been totally, irresistibly responsive when he'd held her, kissed her....

He shivered with the memory. Why not take her to bed and get it over with? Get her out of his system.

Probably all she wanted was to humiliate him by making him lose control.

As it was he was going to have to have a talk with Sharon about his feelings for Carol. It wasn't fair to marry her when his ex-wife still aroused such urgent desire in him. He hadn't been any good for Sharon since the day he'd heard that Carol was coming back. The most he'd been able to manage were brotherly hello and goodbye kisses—and he had to keep reminding himself to do that. He hated the thought of hurting her, but the least he could do was explain the situation and let her make an informed decision about whether or not she wanted to go ahead with the wedding.

Bryce put the tea back in the refrigerator and the rest of the ice cubes in the freezer. Before closing the freezer door he rested his hot forehead against its cold surface. Carol had told him she'd never been unfaithful. If only he could believe her. If she really had settled down as she seemed to have he could forgive her everything but adultery.

Sure, she'd been young and spoiled, Bryce thought, but he hadn't been especially understanding, either. Instead of trying to teach her, help her grow up, he'd nagged her, complained about what a rotten housekeeper she was and pestered her to give him a baby when she wasn't much more than a child herself.

No, he wasn't blameless, but he'd loved her, and it had never even crossed his mind to cheat on her.

He swore and slammed the door shut. What was he thinking? Even if she hadn't actually made love with that junkie, she'd cheated on Bryce just by going out with Joel and hiding it. He didn't want that kind of wife, and no matter how he tried to rationalize it, he knew that if he took her to bed he'd find himself doing whatever was necessary to keep her.

Where was Carol, anyway? It didn't take more than a couple of minutes to explore the house. He walked across the kitchen toward the hall. He'd find her, give her her tea and drive her back to the motel. He had to be crazy to think he could get her out of his system by making love with her.

It was imperative that he get her out of his house and out of his life. Fast!

Carol pressed her lips tightly together in an effort not to cry out her anguish. She was being silly. Why had she expected Bryce to keep the house and furnishings intact, a shrine to her? Actually, now that she thought of it she was surprised he'd even kept the furniture in the front room.

The tearing sobs shook her, and she buried her face deeper in her hands and braced herself against the doorway.

She hadn't heard him coming, but suddenly Bryce's arms were around her, turning her and pressing her face into his shoulder. "Carol. Oh, sweetheart, don't cry." His voice was ragged. "I had no idea coming in the house would upset you so."

His gentle hands caressed her back in a frantic effort to comfort. "I'm sorry. I've been a bastard. I've used you as a whipping boy ever since you came back to Raindance. I don't know what in hell I want."

His arms tightened around her, bringing her flush against his long hard body. "That's not true. I do know what I want. I want you, and it's driving me crazy. I can't think of anything but how soon I can see you again, the way you feel in my arms when I hold you, the euphoria that sings through my blood when our lips meet and you open your mouth for me. Carol, darling, don't cry so! I can't stand it.''

Carol heard the desperation in his voice and wailed all the louder. She wasn't sure whether it was because she was miserable or because she was happy. He was saying the things she'd longed to hear him say, but they were being dragged from him against his will. He sounded angry with himself about wanting her. If only she could convince him to trust her not to hurt him again.

He nibbled the fragrant softness of her neck, and she clasped him to her. ''I love you, Bryce,'' she said through her tears. ''I do. I do. Let me show you how much. I won't ask anything else of you, I promise.''

Without hesitation Bryce lifted her in his arms and walked across the room, where he laid her gently on the unfamiliar bed. The mattress was firm but soft as he followed her down to lie beside her, one of his legs capturing both of hers.

Her heart was pounding and her breath came in short gasps as his mouth claimed hers and their tongues made love. He tasted as she remembered— clean, fresh and male. She combed her fingers through his hair and applied pressure to the back of his head to keep him from raising it. Not that he showed any inclination to do so....

After a while he trailed tiny kisses down her throat and on to the edge of the scooped neckline of her loosely knit top. He pulled the material down and continued across her breastbone, but was stopped again by the lacy top of her bra. ''Let's get some of these clothes off you,'' he said shakily, and quickly disposed of the garments.

They both slipped out of their shoes, and when he had her back in place beneath him he propped himself up on his elbow and looked down at her, his gaze hot and hungry. "I thought you were perfect at twenty, but I didn't realize how much maturity would add to those tantalizing breasts." His voice quivered with desire.

He raised his hand from where it lay on her hip and gently stroked her fullness, sending tremors down her spine. She reached out and started to unbutton his cotton shirt. She could feel his heartbeat accelerate under her hand as he sighed with satisfaction and cupped her tingling breast.

Her hands seemed to be all thumbs as she fumbled with his small buttons, and after the first two she couldn't wait longer to feel his bare skin. She slipped her hand inside and tangled it in the thick blond hair on his chest. He drew in a breath and leaned down to nuzzle the white flesh he was holding in his palm, careful not to interfere with her exploration of him.

Unsatisfied with the limited space she'd uncovered, Carol again tackled the buttons. When she'd finished she pulled the shirt from his jeans and slid it off his shoulders. Her gaze roamed unchecked over his masculine beauty. He'd filled out, too, in the years since she'd last seen him nude. His chest was broader and his shoulders more muscular, but the belly above his low cut jeans was still smooth and fit.

Unable to resist the compulsion she spread her hand there, just below the waist. Her thumb found his navel, and her little finger rubbed against the taut denim below his belt loops.

He squirmed and captured her wayward hand. "Watch where you're putting your hands, honey," he muttered huskily. "I'm having a hard time holding back as it is."

"So am I," she whispered, and gasped as he took her sensitized nipple in his mouth.

She'd forgotten the extent of the effect Bryce's lovemaking had on her, and she tingled all the way to her toes as she arched in reaction. He continued to ravage her breast as he put both hands on her bottom and pulled her against his throbbing need. Then he quickly unfastened the zipper at the back of her shorts and, with fast, jerky movements, slid them down and off, leaving her with only a few inches of bikini panties for covering.

Mindlessly Carol rubbed her palms up and down the flexing muscles of Bryce's back as she put one leg across his hips. He rolled over onto her, and it was evident that he was on the ragged edge of his long-suffering control. Carol reached between them to unfasten the heavy snap at the top of his zipper.

Just as the snap pulled apart the raucous sound of the doorbell penetrated their fog of passion.

They both lurched with surprise, and Bryce muttered a blistering oath as he tightened his hold on her. "We can't stop now!" he groaned.

Carol's whole body screamed in protest, and she wrapped both legs around his hips to hold him closer. "No," she agreed fervently. "Whoever it is will go away in a minute."

The bell rang three more times before it stopped and a pounding on the door began. Bryce swore. "My car's parked in the driveway. Whoever it is knows I must be home."

The pounding stopped, and the unmistakable sound of the door being pushed open was heard instead.

"Son of a—" Bryce jumped from the bed and started toward the bedroom door, which they hadn't bothered to close, when a female voice called "Bryce, are you here?" and a woman appeared in the doorway.

Bryce had just put his hand on the door, and Carol had no way to cover her nudity.

It had been eight years since she'd seen the lady, but even the look of shocked outrage wouldn't disguise the delicate features of Gwen Garrett's face.

Bryce's mother simply stood there and stared, obviously too stunned to move. It was like one of those slow moving nightmares or a film stopped suddenly on the worst possible frame. The spell wasn't broken until a booming male voice called from the porch, "Gwen? Isn't he home? Did you find the key?"

It was Ira Garrett, Bryce's father, and the other three were galvanized into action. Carol crossed her arms over her bare breasts. Gwen turned without a word and fled, and Bryce pushed the door shut. All of them were scarlet with embarrassment.

Carol scampered off the bed and grabbed her clothes while Bryce put on his shirt and refastened his jeans. "I've got to catch them," he said, and hurried from the room, careful to close the door behind him.

Carol was shaking so badly she could hardly dress. Had her sin really been so great that she deserved this kind of punishment? Hadn't she already paid enough by losing Bryce?

She could hear angry voices in the living room and knew she couldn't possibly face Bryce's parents. So she was a coward. She was entitled.

In Los Angeles she was a model of decorum, even a little straitlaced. Not once in her six years at school and two years of working with some of television's flakiest personalities had a hint of scandal touched her, but the minute she set foot in Raindance, Nebraska, she seemed to be embroiled in it.

She had to try three times before her trembling hands could tie her shoes. Then, without even a glance at the door, she opened the old-style sash window that looked out over the backyard, unhooked the screen and climbed out.

The lot wasn't fenced in, and there was a wide alley at the back that bisected the block. A quick glance in all directions convinced Carol she was unobserved, and she walked hurriedly away from the house and down the alley to the street.

She was just in time to see Sharon drive past in her gray Nissan and turn right at the corner, obviously on her way to Bryce's house.

Carol leaned against a convenient tree for support. A thought had just occurred to her that had set her heart rate soaring again. What if Sharon had been a few minutes earlier and had walked in on their lovemaking instead of Mrs. Garrett!

Chapter Ten

Carol didn't hear from Bryce again until six o'clock the next morning. His early call didn't waken her. She'd been too upset to sleep except piecemeal—a few minutes here, an hour there. She was lying in bed staring into the early morning light when the phone rang.

There was no polite greeting. "Carol, can you meet me at my office in half an hour?" His tone was a curious mixture of reluctance and urgency.

"Yes."

"Thank you." The line went dead, and she headed for the shower.

Twenty-five minutes later she knocked on the locked outside door to the law offices and Bryce let her in. He obviously hadn't even been to bed, although he'd shaved and changed clothes. His brown eyes were bleary from lack of sleep, and there were deep grooves in his unnaturally white face. Even his stance was weary and discouraged.

He didn't smile or touch her, but led her into his office and motioned for her to sit down. He perched on the corner of the desk in front of her and rubbed his eyes with his fingertips before he spoke.

"Saying I'm sorry doesn't even come close to what I feel, but it's the best I can come up with. Are you all right? Did you hurt yourself climbing out the window?"

Carol shook her head. "No, it was an easy drop to the ground. I—I'm sorry I deserted you, but I just couldn't face your parents."

"It's just as well you did. We were in the middle of a row when Sharon walked in, too."

"I know," she said. "I was coming out of the alley when I saw her drive by. Oh, Bryce, I'm the one who's sorry. I never should have gone to the house. Now I've really messed things up for you. What happened after I left?"

He slid off the desk and started to pace. "Mom was shocked nearly out of her mind, and when Dad found out what had happened he was furious."

"But it's your house. They shouldn't have barged right in. Even parents have no right to invade their grown son's privacy. Besides, I thought they were in Wyoming."

"They were, but one of Hilary's kids got the chicken pox, so they came home. As for them barging in, it's my own fault. I gave them a key." He plunged his hands in his pockets. "I don't make a habit of bringing women home and making love with them in the middle of the day. You won't believe this, but until you showed up I was an honorable man."

Carol gasped and started to rise. "Oh, Bryce—"

He quickly motioned her to remain seated. "I also have a key to their house," he continued, "and that's what they were after. Mom had left her keys at home and Dad lost his house key somewhere in Wyoming, so they stopped on the way home to get mine. Mom knows where I keep it, so when I didn't answer the doorbell she just assumed I was visiting one of the neighbors and came on in to get it."

Carol slumped back in her seat. "And Sharon?" She wasn't sure she wanted to hear about Sharon.

Bryce's features twisted with anguish. "I would have told her anyway, but to have her come in in the middle of the scene and find out like that..."

He looked so tormented that Carol had to grip the wooden arms of the chair to keep from going to him, taking him in her arms. He'd made it plain that he didn't want any physical contact.

"What are we going to do now?" she asked, her voice a mere whisper.

Bryce turned and walked away from her. "I can't go on like this, Carol. It's like walking around with a knife in my gut and wondering why I hurt. My judgment, my sense of fair play—even my integrity—desert me when I get you within touching distance."

He paused by the window. "Up until now I've considered myself reasonably bright. I was in the top five percent of my law class and graduated with honors. But there's a part of me, the male part, that will always be in bondage to you. I thought I'd finally conquered that. I even believed my feelings for Sharon were strong enough that we could marry and be happy together. I knew I didn't love her with the fire and passion with which I'd loved you, but she was special to me. Our interests were the same, and she was most of the things I wanted in a wife.''

Carol fidgeted as his words cloaked her in forboding. Jim Perkins had been right after all. She could never make Bryce happy. He wouldn't allow himself to trust her ever again.

He took a deep breath and turned to face her. ''I'm going to do what I should have done days ago. I'm going to ask you to leave Raindance—today, if possible. Tom and I can easily handle the sale of your mother's property. There's no need for you to stay. I've always known that, and still I've kept you here. Now I've hurt Sharon, and I never, ever intended to do that.''

Carol knew the crushing weight of despair. She'd lost her last opportunity to convince Bryce she loved him and could be the wife he needed. He wasn't willing to gamble, and she couldn't blame him. He wanted her physically, but the love he'd once felt for her was gone and couldn't be revived. She prayed she hadn't ruined his chance to make a new life with Sharon Davis.

Carol dampened her dry lips with the tip of her tongue. ''Wh-what about Sharon? Did she break your engagement?''

He shrugged. ''She didn't throw the ring back in my face and call me dirty names, if that's what you mean. I almost wish she had. It would have been better than having to watch her trust and respect for me shatter. She left the house as soon as she realized what the commotion was about, and when she finally agreed to talk to me later in the evening nothing was settled. She didn't even call me a bastard, she just looked through me like I wasn't there.''

His tone was filled with pain and regret.

"Do you still want to marry her?"

He nodded. "Yes. If she'll still have me. I'm not a swinging bachelor. I need a wife and family. I've been lonely long enough."

Carol winced. He couldn't have put it any more clearly. He wanted a wife, and he wanted that wife to be Sharon, not her. Well, she'd caused him enough grief. She wasn't going to make a fool of herself by begging for a place in his life.

She stood and reached to pick up her purse. "Your parents? Did you manage to calm them down?"

He raised his hands, palms up, in a gesture of yet another defeat. "Mom went home with a migraine and Dad said he hoped I hadn't gotten you pregnant."

Involuntarily her fingers touched her stomach. If only he had. At least then she'd have some part of him. She wondered if he'd told his Dad that their rotten timing had prevented any possibility of that.

She walked toward the door in the deserted office suite, and Bryce followed silently. How did she say goodbye to the man who meant more to her than anything else in life? She'd been spared that the first time. He'd taken her to her parents' home and dumped her without a word. She hadn't seen him again. When she'd left town several days later he'd been nowhere around.

Now as he held the door open she turned and looked at him. Their gazes met and melded, and the bittersweet tension between them was agony. Didn't her love for him shine from her eyes? His were clouded, unreadable. If he regretted sending her away again he didn't let it show.

She started to put her hand out to touch him, but caught it in time to stop. In the end she just walked hurriedly off without either of them saying anything.

Carol's first inclination was to throw her clothes in the car and leave town immediately, but by the time she'd driven the length of Main Street and down Highway 20 to the motel she was too heartsick either to make decisions or to act on them.

She sat in the uncomfortable chair in her room for a long time, dazed and defeated. She hadn't come to Raindance with any hope of reconciling with Bryce, but once she'd seen him that hope had sprung to life without her encouragement. All along Bryce had been telling her he wouldn't take her back, but his actions had sent mixed signals and she'd been foolish enough to respond to the passion rather than the contempt.

Finally the numbness wore off, but with her returning awareness came the surge of pain she'd known was there in hiding, waiting to hit full force. It was then she started packing. Thank heaven she really had come home from Rosemarie's night before last and done her hand laundry.

Rosemarie. Carol had promised to see her again before leaving town. The last thing she wanted to do was say goodbye to anybody, but she might never see Rosie again. They'd grown up together and had shared a special bond of friendship during those years that was rare and special. She owed it to herself and to Rosie not to walk away again without a word.

She looked at her watch. It was nearly noon, and she hadn't had breakfast. Maybe Rosemarie could get away and meet her somewhere for lunch. She could bring the children along if she couldn't get a sitter.

Carol picked up the phone and dialed the Perkinses' number. Rosemarie was delighted with the invitation to lunch and assured Carol there was a high-school girl next door who would baby-sit. They agreed to meet at the Steak and Stein in half an hour.

Carol was waiting at a table when Rosemarie walked in. After one look at Carol her big smile disappeared as she slid into the booth on the opposite side of the table.

"Tell me what's wrong," she said, with more perception than Carol had expected.

"I'm going back to California this afternoon, and I wanted to see you again before I left."

"And what about Bryce?"

Carol's head jerked up with surprise. Surely Rosie wasn't implying what she seemed to be. "What about him?"

Rosemarie sighed. "Oh, come off it, Carol. When you and Bryce are in the same room it's like standing in front of an open furnace. The two of you positively radiate heat. Are you telling me he's going to let you go again?"

Carol could see it was long past time for her to leave town. "Yes, he's letting me leave. He's engaged to Sharon, remember?"

Rosemarie opened her mouth to retort, but Carol touched her hand and shook her head. "Please, do me a favor and don't talk about Bryce. Let's just have this one last lunch for old times' sake before we're separated again."

Rosie nodded, but her expression was filled with compassion.

Two hours later they said goodbye with hugs, a few tears and promises to stay in touch this time.

Carol changed into comfortable well-worn jeans and a sleeveless shirt and continued packing. If she could leave by four o'clock she'd get to North Platte before she stopped for the night.

She was folding dresses into the suitcase when there was a knock on the door. She'd called the office and asked that her bill be figured, and she assumed it was being brought to her.

She opened the door and found herself face-to-face with Sharon Davis.

Sharon was the last person Carol had either expected or wanted to see again, and for a moment they just stood there looking at each other. Finally, Carol found her voice. "Sharon? Won't you come in?"

Sharon nodded and walked past Carol, then turned as Carol shut the door. She didn't waste time on small talk. "I had lunch with Bryce, and he tells me you're leaving."

She was positively bristling with anger, which Carol could understand, yet she seemed upset that Carol was leaving. It didn't make sense.

"Yes. I'll be packed and ready to go in just a few minutes."

"Do you get your kicks out of making Bryce fall in love with you and then walking out on him?" Her sarcasm was heavy and uncharacteristic.

Carol was dumbfounded. "He doesn't want me, he wants you. He told me so."

"And if he told you pigs can fly would you believe him? Good Lord, Carol, how can an intelligent woman like you be so dense? If he was making love with you as passionately as Gwen Garrett seems to think he was, what makes you think he's changed his mind today?''

This couldn't be happening. Sweet, calm Sharon couldn't be raging at her like this. Besides, she was championing the wrong cause. "We weren't—''

"Oh, yes you were," she interrupted savagely. "You might not have completed the encounter, but you were making love. Don't argue semantics with me—I'm a schoolteacher. Bryce never stopped loving you. I've always known that, even if he didn't. I agreed to marry him anyway, because I thought I could make him forget you, but then you had to come back and get him all riled up again.''

Sharon's fists clenched and unclenched at her sides, and her soft, ladylike voice had risen several decibels. "I love Bryce," she declared flatly. "Oh, there aren't any fireworks between us, but we were good together, and I'm not going to let you hurt him again.''

"But he's engaged to you!''

"Not anymore, and don't be so damn noble. If you want him you'll have to go after him and make him see that you two can be happy together. He won't come to you. You hurt him too badly. He won't leave himself vulnerable to that kind of torture again unless you don't give him a choice.''

She turned away, but her tone was challenging. "Have you really grown up, Carol, or don't you have the guts and maturity to fight for what you want?''

Carol was amazed at the tiger that had emerged from the pussycat she'd thought Sharon to be. There was an iron will under that soft exterior.

Carol was loath to hurt the other woman, but she had to acknowledge Sharon was right. Carol and Bryce had a strong, magnetic bond of love that wouldn't be denied, and neither of them could be truly happy without the other.

"Are you sure this is what you want?" she asked.

Sharon faced her again and managed a small smile. "It may not be what I want, but it's what I'm going to get. I couldn't live with Bryce knowing he was yearning for you."

"You're some lady." Carol's voice was tinged with respect. "I wish we could have been friends."

"Don't canonize me just yet," Sharon replied briskly. "I'm not going to pine away in the name of unrequited love. I've had an offer to join a team of teachers who are setting up a school in one of the underdeveloped parts of Mexico, and I'm going to accept. I minored in foreign languages in college, and this is something I've wanted to do. I had decided to turn it down, but now that I won't be getting married I can make better use of my second love, teaching."

She walked to the door and opened it, then turned back. Her lovely face bore marks of the strain she was under.

"I wish we could have been friends, too," she murmured, then left, closing the door behind her.

Carol felt drained. If there were any more shocks in store for her today she wasn't sure she could survive them.

She looked at the empty suitcase on the bed and at the dresses waiting to be put in it. Was she up to another session with Bryce—and the almost certain rejection that would follow? How much could her poor battered emotions stand? Wouldn't it be easier just to leave town and not have to endure the humiliation of throwing herself at him and being rejected yet again?

Sure it would, she realized, but who said she was entitled to easy? She had a lot to make up for, and she owed it to both Bryce and herself to make one last effort at a reconciliation now that Sharon had broken the engagement. Even if he refused to listen to her or threw her out of the house, at least she would have made the attempt.

She dialed his office, identified herself and asked for Bryce. Surprisingly, Lila put her right through. When he picked up the phone he sounded harried.

"This is Carol," she said, and heard his quick intake of breath. "I'm packed and ready to leave, but something has come up and I need to see you."

There was a long pause at the other end. "I don't like goodbyes," he said finally, his voice ragged.

"Neither do I, and I promise not to say it. Can you meet me at your house when you're through there?"

"Why can't you come to the office?"

She gripped the phone and wished she'd never started this. "Please, Bryce." She knew she was pleading.

Another hesitation. "All right," he said. "Half an hour." They both hung up.

She finished packing and checked out of the motel. No matter what happened in the next hour or so, she wouldn't be coming back.

Exactly thirty minutes after she'd spoken to Bryce, Carol drove up and parked in front of his house.

Bryce answered the bell still dressed in his suit trousers and dress shirt, although he'd removed his tie and unbuttoned his collar. He stood in the doorway, blocking it. "Are you going to cry?" he asked grimly.

Carol blinked. "No, I promise." Her voice was a whisper.

He stood back to allow her to enter, then ushered her into the living room and motioned her to sit down. He continued to stand. Carol continued to stand, too.

She twisted the strap of her purse nervously. "Sharon came to see me," she said.

He leaned against the wall and folded his arms across his chest. His face was expressionless. "Oh?"

Carol nodded. "She was very angry at me—not because I'd been caught making love with her fiancé, but because I was going back to California."

A brief flash of surprise crossed Bryce's grim features, but he remained silent.

"She said you two were no longer engaged."

Still no reaction from Bryce.

Carol swallowed. "She said you're...you're still in love with me."

He didn't move a muscle, just stood there glaring at her. She could feel beads of sweat on her forehead. "Bryce, I know you still have feelings for me. Maybe not love, but every time we're together there's a potent awareness between us. You feel it as strongly as I do."

It was like pleading her case before a statue. Was he even hearing anything she said?

She turned away, unable to continue looking at him. "I know you don't believe I wasn't sleeping with Joel, but it's the truth. You're the only man I've ever wanted to make love with, the only man I've ever slept with."

The continued silence clawed at her raw nerve ends, and she thought she'd scream before he finally spoke. "Why should I believe you? You've lied to me in the past and taken advantage of my love to get what you wanted."

He didn't sound forgiving.

"I know." Carol's voice was laced with defeat. "I just hoped that maybe... Sharon said I should fight for you, make you take me back."

"So why don't you?"

She jumped and turned to face him, sure she hadn't heard him right. He hadn't moved. Both his look and his stance were forbidding.

She licked her lips. "I—I don't know how."

"You could start by touching me."

Her eyes widened. Was he putting her on? He looked as if he'd bite if she tried to touch him.

She walked slowly toward him. "Where?"

He shrugged nonchalantly. "It doesn't matter. Wherever you want."

She almost smiled at the mental picture that invitation created, but she was afraid. He wasn't giving her any clues about what he had in mind.

She reached up and put her palm against his cheek. It was bristly with five o'clock shadow, and a muscle twitched. A good sign?

Slowly she slid her hand upward and ran her fingers through his slightly rumpled hair as she put her other hand on his shoulder and kneaded gently.

"I'm a sucker for a kiss," he informed her brusquely.

She stood on her toes and pushed his head down so she could plant a moist kiss on his forehead, then either cheek and the indentation in his chin. She couldn't get closer to him because he still had his arms crossed on his chest, but she managed to brush her lips down his throat and nibble on the sensitive spot beneath his ear.

With a low groan he uncrossed his arms and clasped them around her waist pulling her hard against him. She looked up and saw there were tears in his eyes.

"Oh, my darling," she murmured before his mouth claimed hers and everything else was forgotten in the tumult.

They clung to each other as their tears and lips intermingled, and then, without breaking the kiss, he slid his arm under her knees and picked her up. He carried her to the bedroom and kicked the door shut with a slam behind them.

She wasn't sure how they got undressed, but then they were lying on the cool white sheets, their hands caressing each other, their bodies closely entwined.

"My beautiful, bewitching wife," he said huskily between kisses. "I never stopped loving you. It's not possible. Oh, Carol, love me, let me love you."

"You don't need to ask," she moaned, and opened to receive him. To become one with him in body and soul and to accept him again as lover, husband, friend.

A long time later, after their ardor had cooled to something slightly less explosive, they lay wrapped in each other's arms. Carol was lying where she had collapsed on top of him after yet another earth-shattering release, and his hand roamed absently over her bare bottom.

"Am I too heavy for you?" she murmured into his chest.

"Not a chance. I adore every ounce of that hot little body of yours," he answered with sleepy contentment. "I'll never get enough of you. We'll be remarried as soon as we can get a license, but it's only a legal formality. In my heart you've always been my wife, and you always will be."

She sighed happily. "Do you really mean that, or are you just saying it to please me?"

"I don't have to make up things to please you, sweetheart. All I have to do is put into words what I feel. I've loved you all my life. Not because I wanted to, but because it was something I had no control over.

"We won't dwell on the past eight years, but for me they were pure, unadulterated hell, because in spite of what I thought you'd done I wanted you, needed you, loved you."

She raised her head to reassure him, but he put his finger to her mouth. "It's over now, and I don't want to hear any more about it. When you walked in the house this afternoon we started a new life. The past is dead and buried, but we do have to talk about the future."

Carol's muscles tensed with alarm. "We do?"

Bryce nodded. "There's the little matter of where we're going to live."

She frowned. "Aren't we going to live here?"

He turned so that she slid off him and lay on her back with him reclining next to her on his side, his head propped in his hand. "You have a career in Los Angeles. Your home's there. Your mother and your friends are there. Are you willing to give all that up to return to Raindance?"

Carol turned her head and kissed his flat nipple. "If Raindance is where you are then that's where I want to be."

He opened his mouth to protest, but this time she put her finger to his lips. "No, Bryce, listen to me. I'm glad I have my education and that I've been a success in my chosen career, but now it's time to go on to another phase of my life. I don't want to be Ms. Carol

Murphy, public relations executive, anymore. I want
to be Mrs. Bryce Garrett, wife and mother. I want babies, darling, and we should start having them soon.''

Bryce's expression was a mixture of elation and
alarm. "Carol, I was unreasonable before when I insisted we have a baby. You're not the only one who
grew up in the intervening years. I know now that not
all women want the hassle and responsibility of raising children. That was brought home most graphi-
cally a few nights ago when Rosemarie ran away from
Jim. I don't intend to make the same mistake he did.
I don't need babies, but I do need you."

She put out her hand and caressed his troubled face.
"And I need you, but I'd like to have sons and
daughters, too. I want to be there when they get their
first tooth, take their first step, say their first word. I
want to join the hospital auxiliary and be president of
the PTA. But most of all I want to have time for loving you."

Bryce made a purring sound deep in his throat and
leaned his face into her caressing hand. "But Rosemarie—"

"Rosie's problem is a valid one, but it's not mine.
She wanted independence and a career, but instead she
married right out of college and immediately started
a family. Now she's pregnant with her third child and
it seems to her she'll be tied down to diapers and preschool forever. It's good that she and Jim are finally
getting counseling. They need it."

She put her arms around his neck and pulled him
down so she could kiss him. They got lost in the
magic, and it was a while before they spoke again.

"Now, what were we talking about?" she asked
softly. "Oh yes, my dreams were totally different than

Rosemarie's. All I ever wanted was to be your wife. I had no career ambitions, and even though I did resist the idea of having a baby when we were first married I always intended to have a family later."

He still looked puzzled. "I thought all women wanted to be liberated."

Carol laughed. "I am liberated, love. I'll be doing exactly what I want to do. That's what liberation for women is all about. I'm free to make my own choices, and I opt for being a full-time wife and mother. If Rosie wants a career then she should be able to have it without feeling guilty. Do you understand what I'm saying?"

Bryce nuzzled her soft breast. "I understand that you want the same things I do, and we'll sort out the rest of it later."

She stroked his head as it lay between her breasts. "Some day when I'm no longer needed full-time at home, I'll want to go back to work again. I think I'd like to work with you. Could you put up with me as your legal assistant?"

He chuckled and gently rubbed her bare thigh. "You've got to be kidding. Maybe in twenty-five or thirty years I'll be able to work with you in the same office without being totally distracted by that swishy little gluteus maximus of yours, but don't count on it."

The grin disappeared and he was serious once more. "I'm a damn good attorney, and although I like Raindance I'm not committed to it. If you ever get bored and want to move to a city where you can get back into public relations again, just say so. I can practice law anywhere."

Bryce's arms tightened around her. "Just don't ever leave me again."

He kissed her, and Carol snuggled into his embrace.

She'd been given a chance to return to Raindance, her yesterday, and make all their tomorrows shining and bright. And this time she knew she could make it happen.

*   *   *   *   *

Come back to Raindance and share in Carol and Bryce's happily-ever-after... when handsome, incorrigible
Rusty Watt asks them for help with a problem involving the town's lovely new librarian—in
RAINDANCE AUTUMN,
available in June.
Don't miss it!

COMING NEXT MONTH

#568 JACINTH—Laurey Bright
Lovely Jacinth Norwood wouldn't let a man inside her secret world, but Mark
Harding knew he belonged there. His passion for her was growing—could it
melt her icy shell?

#569 THE TAKEOVER MAN—Frances Lloyd
When she bumped into the new director of promotion, advertising executive
Kate Camilleri thought she'd never met a more infuriating man—or a more
handsome one. Nick Wedderburn's charm might burn her in the end, but Kate
didn't care—he could set her heart on fire....

#570 A HALF-DOZEN REASONS—Darlene Patten
Grant Russell was what Karen Wagner had always wanted—affectionate, funny
and powerfully attractive. But he was the father of six children! Karen had
never seen herself as Maria von Trapp, but she'd climb every mountain to find
her dream with Grant.

#571 SOMEDAY MY LOVE—Patti Beckman
When Dak Roberts left town to become an Olympic star, he vowed he'd return
to Kathy Ayers someday. That day had come—Dak looked at Kathy and knew,
for the first time in his life, he was really home....

#572 POPCORN AND KISSES—Kasey Michaels
Theater manager Sharon Wheeler loved the romance of the old drive-in, but
Zachary St. Clair, head of the corporation, thought she was living in the past.
He was profits and losses while she was popcorn and kisses. Would the future
bring them together?

#573 BABY MAKES THREE—Sharon De Vita
What could be better than a man who'd won a Mother of the Year award?
Maggie Magee had never thought about it—until she met "Wild Bill" Cody
and his little son, Bobby. Now Maggie wanted to win the greatest prize of all—
Cody's heart.

AVAILABLE THIS MONTH:

#562 IF YOU LOVE ME
Joan Smith

#563 SOMETHING GOOD
Brenda Trent

#564 THE SWEETHEART WALTZ
Susan Kalmes

#565 THE MAN OF HER DREAMS
Glenda Sands

#566 RETURN TO RAINDANCE
Phyllis Halldorson

#567 SOME KIND OF WONDERFUL
Debbie Macomber

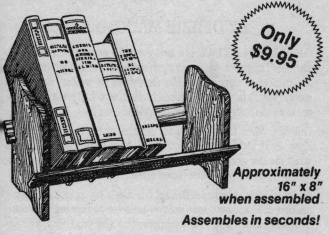

Silhouette Romance™

Legendary Lovers Trilogy

BY DEBBIE MACOMBER....

ONCE UPON A TIME, in a land not so far away, there lived a girl, Debbie Macomber, who grew up dreaming of castles, white knights and princes on fiery steeds. Her family was an ordinary one with a mother and father and one wicked brother, who sold copies of her diary to all the boys in her junior high class.

One day, when Debbie was only nineteen, a handsome electrician drove by in a shiny black convertible. Now Debbie knew a prince when she saw one, and before long they lived in a two-bedroom cottage surrounded by a white picket fence.

As often happens when a damsel fair meets her prince charming, children followed, and soon the two-bedroom cottage became a four-bedroom castle. The kingdom flourished and prospered, and between soccer games and car pools, ballet classes and clarinet lessons, Debbie thought about love and enchantment and the magic of romance.

One day Debbie said, "What this country needs is a good fairy tale." She remembered how well her diary had sold and she dreamed again of castles, white knights and princes on fiery steeds. And so the stories of Cinderella, Beauty and the Beast, and Snow White were reborn....

Look for Debbie Macomber's *Legendary Lovers* trilogy from Silhouette Romance: *Cindy and the Prince* (January, 1988); *Some Kind of Wonderful* (March, 1988); *Almost Paradise* (May, 1988). Don't miss them!

SRT-1